Meant to Dance

Meant to Dance

Sonya Behan

Adam & Deb—
My teachers, parents
and greatest resource.
Thank you for helping
me grow and find my
voice.
Love Sonya

RADIANT HEART PRESS

Milwaukee, Wisconsin

Published by
Radiant Heart Press
An imprint of HenschelHAUS Publishing, Inc.
www.henschelhausbooks.com

ISBN: 978159598-086-1
E-ISBN: 978159598-457-9
LCCN: 2016933526

Printed in the United States of America

This book is dedicated to my children.
May you learn how great love is and can be.

The O'Neill Family Tree

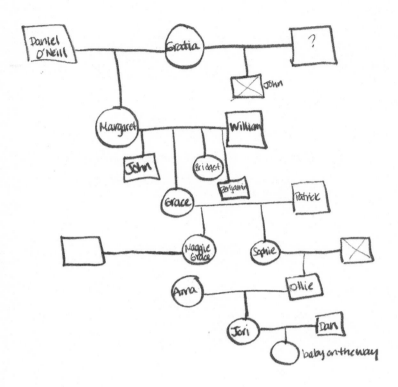

Prologue

*W*ith a slight sigh, I had let that very confusing and painful time arrive back into my consciousness. Like the slow steady wind blowing through the various crevices of a forest path, searching for just the right place to pause for a rest, my mind sifts through remnants of a time long past.

The times and places drift by swiftly and I hope that I too will come to a place of rest that will provide some peace of mind and clarity for the questions I seem to ask daily now.

There is so much I don't understand after seeing Aidan today for the first time in almost seventy years. At least that is how long I think it has been. I am not entirely sure. I am so confused by the memory lapses I seem to have when trying to recall events and experiences I have had throughout my life. At times, a memory is quite clear and I don't question its presence. But there are situations like today when I can't recall when I last saw Aidan, but I can remember where. I also realize I can't recall my son Ollie's time in college or when he met his wife. It wasn't that long ago, was it?

I decided that if my granddaughter Jori felt that reading some of my journals would help her, then perhaps they could do the same for me.

Opening a journal from my early adolescence, I am immediately smiling at the doodles and quotes from various writers, family members, friends and movies that had caught my interest. I had pressed flowers from summer and leaves from the autumn. My two favorite seasons. Especially during the time of late summer and early autumn when the air begins to cool and the leaves turn to orange, yellow and red. That time of year is so magical for me, especially when the skies seem to glow at night as the sun sets and you can still hear the crickets.

Wary from trying to force the answers I seek, I finally close my eyes and take a few deep steady breaths. I surrender and allow the anxiety knotted within my stomach to loosen. Unraveling the many choices I made throughout my life, I begin to see one particular picture in my mind.

I take another deep breath in and then another. With each new breath, I able to see the memory come slowly into focus. Yes, there I am … standing in the rain watching him walk away.

Part One

Morning

6 a.m.

Sophie

You haven't left my mind, not even for a second.

Those words have come to me three times in my life. The first time they were written, the second in way of traveling on invisible threads hundreds of miles away, and the third time today in person.

Despite the apparent infrequency of their expression, they have sat within my heart and spirit for more than seven decades. Their message still touches my heart in many mysterious and wonderful ways. They do not age, even though looking at me today, you might think I have. But that would limit you to what you can see only with your eyes.

I am filled with gratitude at having reached the grand age of ninety-three. It is a gift, as each year has been since my birth. Of course, I didn't always feel that way and on the mornings I wake up stiff or when Jori, my lovely granddaughter, insists I stop dipping the peanut butter on my spoon into my chocolate chips because it is not healthy, I admit it feels hard to accept my age. My hair is still long, although no longer touched with light golden-brown highlights as it was when I was a much younger woman.

In fact, it is almost entirely white, with only very slight remnants of my youth. My once slim fingers are disfigured with arthritis. It is a periodic reminder of the years that I have spent here on The Hill working hard to ensure it remain the sanctuary I grew up with, the one I feel it is today, and the legacy that Jori will carry forward. Although my fingers are stiff and slightly curved between my joints, I enjoy running my fingers through my hair and over my favorite dragonfly clip.

Today, my hand finds a place to rest in the center of my chest as I allow those words to enter and remind me of how they changed the course of my life. They provided the door through which I found myself walking time and time again. Each time, they offered me a way to see how the choice I made to let Aidan go was one from which I never recovered.

I see now that my own personal truths about the choice I made to let Aidan go and allow Ollie's father to take his place would irrevocably change not only my life, but Ollie's and Jori's, too.

I had no idea just how much I had agreed to learn about love during this life time. I suppose if I had, I might have done a better job at running to avoid the pain, the grief, and the impatience I had with the process. If I had been successful, I certainly would have lost the ability to forgive myself and others. Most importantly, I would never have had Ollie in my life. He is the best and purest love I have ever known. For this reason alone, I have no regrets about loving another.

"*You haven't left my mind, not even for a second.*" Hearing myself say those words aloud allows them to linger.

They are embedded in my heart with an imprint that would lead me to the truth about how I have struggled with and learned about love.

After so many years of not thinking of them, they somehow seem to carry the same intense energy despite the long-ago connection. Those ten words shaped so much of where I have been and the life I led that I am sometimes stopped with sudden astonishment as to how much they have given me. Interesting how words can leave an unspeakable impact on us; like the wind, we breathe them in giving us life with their energy. We don't always feel them, but they are nestled deep within the center of our very being.

How do words do that? How can they carry so much meaning when seemingly only written to express affection to another? How can they have given so much to me in ways that are practically indescribable?

Despite this latest review of my past, I feel comfortable in my favorite chair by the window on this slightly cool summer morning. I feel the imprint left so long ago in my heart for the first time. I notice that the sun has found its place to rise and the stillness of the deeply wooded dawn has provided a sense of solitude and peace.

The beautiful song of morning birds creates a melody I absolutely love. It is perfect for a stroll through the orchard.

I sense that today holds something special, something I will never forget. Much like the one I have replayed many times in my mind since I was fourteen, standing in the rain, feeling it pour over my eyes, down my arms, and into the puddle enveloping my feet.

In my thoughts, I must have watched Aiden and me laugh, play, and swirl around thousands of times. My memories have provided me solace, joy, and at times, sorrow.

Perhaps there's something in the air this morning. I feel different today. Can't tell you why exactly.

9 a.m.

*W*hen I woke up this morning, I thought my day was just going to be centered around some drawing and perhaps taking a nap or two under the trees. I can't physically continue with my stained glass work anymore, so drawing is the next best thing I could be doing.

The day has become bumpy—that is, for Jori. I found her in the baby's nursery talking to herself and then trying to find me to talk to, as well.

For whatever reason, Jori felt that digging through our old journals and talking to me would give her the answers about herself she so desperately longed to find. Watching her trying to reach deep in the trunk over her watermelon-sized stomach was both comical and sad.

I knew all too well the struggle she was experiencing— the desperate ways the women in our family forced the answers to resolve whatever issue they had with exhaustive analysis, mixed with unrealistic timeframes in which to feel better.

Let's not forget the pride and strain of stubbornness that has lasted throughout the generations. Perhaps there would be something one of the Apple Tree Warriors, as we called ourselves, could offer something that would assist our dear Jori. It's just that I had learned long ago that the answers to one's questions would only come when you are ready for them.

With enough time and patience, the answers always reveal themselves. Neither I nor the other women in our family could give Jori exactly what she was looking for. Most certainly, the answer about whether she should remain married to Dan would not come by analyzing the choices I myself had made long ago.

Observing her for what felt like hours, and then hearing her eventually call out to me, I realized that although I could not directly give her the reprieve she craved, I could perhaps guide her to at least one journal to start with that could possibly provide some relief. If we were lucky, maybe some clarity, too.

Truth be told, listening to her rant agitated me and I decided it was time to help Jori snap out of this latest whirlwind of self-pity. Breaking the quietness in the air, I used my firmest voice with her.

"Of course, we know you need us! For God's sake, Jori, stop feeling sorry for yourself!" Seeing that it gave Jori the needed jolt, I continued by pointing to the purple journal tucked below several other journals.

Startled, but with some clear relief in her voice, Jori replies, "Grandma, I had no idea you were already here."

"Well, if you hadn't been sniffling so much and making so much noise trying to find my journals, you would have known that I have been standing here for quite some time now. In fact, it feels like hours."

I can see that Jori feels disgruntled and hurt by the way I have snapped at her.

"I don't need your lectures right now, Sophie!" Jori retorts defiantly.

"Of course you do, Jori, because you have gotten yourself all worked up and are not even paying attention to the answers already right in front of you. You can't look for your answers by being afraid and trying to live your answers through my life."

Jori's eyes close and I see her fight the wincing that has naturally formed on her face in acknowledgement that what I have said is true. Her face remains tight, a reflection of just how hard it is for her to hear the truth.

"I am not trying to live my answers through your life, Grandma. I just don't want to make the same mistakes you did." In a calmer voice, Jori continues to explain that she only wants what's best for the baby and doesn't want what happened to her father to happen to her child.

I am stunned. How in the world did she draw the conclusion that what is happening between her and Dan was anything like what Ollie's dad and I went through? I know that Ollie's dad and I had some rough moments. Certainly the last one had ended with Ollie never seeing his father again, but Dan would never do that to Jori. Ollie's father was a different man. She really shouldn't compare the two.

"Jori, Dan is nothing like Ollie's father was. I don't believe Dan will break your heart."

Jori stays silent for a minute or so before she looks up at me. Softly she says, "Grandma, I don't think you remember everything. In fact, I know you don't. Dad always said you never recovered from the night his father never came back, because it reminded you too much of what happened to you and Aunt Maggie Grace. I have not been sure that was true until now. I see it in your eyes and hear it when you talk about *him.*"

"Well, I don't know what to say about that, Jori, I guess everyone has a right to their opinions." I am saddened and a feeling of uneasiness rises from what she has said, but there must be a reason for her to be so sure about my recollection of Ollie's father, or more accurately, what happened between us. I should probably follow up with Ollie about this. Damn, my memory just isn't what it was.

I redirect Jori back to the journals and she scans the trunk where the leather-bound books are stacked awkwardly on top of one another. Amidst the hundred or more years of personal exploration, Jori's eyes finally lock onto the journal I pointed out earlier, and she releases a quick sigh. It's a relief to me to see her finally be able to breathe in a relaxed manner.

Slowly, she picks up my journal and stands again, despite the strain of the baby's weight. Then she plops down in her Great-Aunt Maggie Grace's rocking chair. For a moment, I see her holding her breath in hopeful anticipation of what she believes she will find.

Slowly, I walk over and lean over the back of the rocker. I let myself again drift back to that summer night's rain when I was just fourteen. I can still smell the lilacs and apples embedded in the pages. I am now convinced this is the right journal for Jori to begin her exploration.

"I hope this helps, Jori. I will be back if you need me."

Smiling, she opens the journal as I walk away. For a few moments, I stay to watch Jori through the doorway. She continues to rock gently as she gently turns the pages to read the journal.

Cautiously making my way down the worn stairway, I begin to let myself drift softly back to my experience as a young girl, trying so hard to be a woman.

10 a.m.

Jori

This morning has been tough. I haven't been able to sleep for weeks. The baby kicks and moves around a lot now, especially at night.

Barely able to bend over anymore now that my belly has grown enormously with my first child, I begin to take in that she is due to be born in only a few short weeks. I can't help but place my face in my hands and cry. I'm so tired of feeling confused.

I am tired of trying to find clues from a woman—well, let me rephrase that—from ALL the crazy women in this family, when what I need to know most is that I am going to be okay! Can't they understand that? Why does this have to be so hard?!

In a barely audible whisper, I send a plea to my grandmother. "Don't you know how much I need you? And the rest of the O'Neill women?"

When I murmured those words, I had no idea that Sophie was looking at me and seeing the many times that not only she, but the other women in our family, had planted their faces in their hands, wet from crying and feeling scared, lonely, and unsure about what their next step would be.

Having Grandma Sophie with me was often comforting, but it could be challenging, too. I know she means well when she speaks candidly to me, but sometimes her delivery stings me. Hard.

I know she cares, as do they all, but Sophie has always been with me. She has spent practically every day of my life with me since I was born. Amazing when I think about it. Not even my parents spent almost every day with me. And when they did, it wasn't like being with Grandma Sophie.

Growing up, I saw Great-Aunt Maggie Grace weekly and of course, all the other extended members of my family at least one to two times a month. I guess some may say that we are close. It's just what we did—gathered together. It didn't matter who was getting along with whom. Every Saturday and Sunday was spent on The Hill, eating, talking and playing games together. Of course, there was drinking, too.

So many disputes were resolved over croquet in the summer, apple picking in the fall, ice skating/hockey in the winter, and pig roasts in the spring. Depending on the weather, we also snow-shoed, skied, and took late-night swims in the O'Neill pond. Our family did all sorts of fun things year round, regardless of our circumstances or life situations. No one was ever turned away. No one was ever made to feel they were not worthy of spending time on The Hill.

We don't always get along, That would simply not be realistic for such a strong-willed, tougher-than-nails kind of family. Our self-determination and work ethic are our greatest gifts and weaknesses. I know for a fact that regardless of how emotionally I am connected to someone in the family, any one of them would come to my aid if I needed anything at all. Anytime. For any reason. But don't misunderstand loyalty for enabling anyone.

Let me make one thing very clear. In our family, if you mess up, you will hear about it for the rest of your life. And you are expected to get yourself out of any mess you got yourself into. It was that simple. I guess this is the family's way of making sure you don't mess up again in the same way. You get one chance to learn and then…well, I don't want to know what happens. I have never been told more than once to figure out my crap.

Now feeling more comforted and reading through the journal Grandma directed me to this morning, I can perhaps understand more of what she wanted me to know. Wiping away the tears of self-pity that have moistened my cheeks and run down my neck, I take a deep breath in, as if I am trying to deflate the puffiness in my face.

I already know she is right about how futile it is for me to demand answers for my situation with Dan by feeling sorry for myself and expecting others to point out the answers that can only come from me. I just want some sort of light—guidance, if you will—so that I can feel more sure of my next step. Having this baby has brought so much joy and yet created so much anxiety within me. Am I really ready to pass on the O'Neill legacy to my yet-unborn daughter?

Placing the journal on the small table near the chair I have set up for the baby's arrival in the next couple of weeks, I sit down. My back is starting to ache from trying to balance the weight of the baby's growth and the needs of my spine to remain in alignment.

Staring at the journal, I barely noticed Sophie's exit. I bring the journal to what remains of my lap to begin reading again. Amazingly, the scent of lilacs and apples rises from the pages. It is a scent Sophie not only grew up with, but one we all know intimately since it has permeated every board in our family home. Lilacs and apples have been a part of this family, so long that it is no wonder it fills the air even when neither is growing.

Feeling the journal on my lap, smelling the sweet, earthy scent it gives off, I can quickly imagine my grandmother being at the age where she is still a young girl, but trying to be a young woman.

Opening her journal is something I don't do lightly. These are my grandmother's innermost thoughts and I respect her greatly. I am immediately captivated by her art. It tells me about her emotions and thoughts with the various colors she has placed on the page.

I love the way Grandma doodled and provided small glimpses of what she wanted to say on that particular day and time. She was—and is—such a wonderful inspiration!

Opening up this glimpse into the past has calmed me considerably. I am excited to find out what lies among these pages and am extraordinarily mindful of the fact that that with each swirl of paint, marker, pencil and pen, I am looking intimately at my own grandmother's deepest feelings and thoughts. I am not so sure just any granddaughter would have this kind of opportunity. I am deeply grateful and somewhat surprised that Grandma would let me do this. In some regards, she is a very open and candid person, but in other ways, she is incredibly guarded and not easy to understand.

As I begin to take in the first page, I immediately realize that this is the beginning of Sophie and Aidan's story. Wow! She does know me so well! It can't be a coincidence that she met Aidan at the same age I met Dan. It can't be a coincidence that she KNOWS that the beginning of their story will help me understand mine. No wonder she stopped talking and had become so impatient with me! Her words, written so many years ago, have already said it (at least I hope this is the case).

I see a pressed daisy, a stalk of dried lavender, and a leaf from a springtime lilac bush on her first entry. Her handwriting looks like it is dancing with the ways she has twirled the ends of some of the letters—like her y's and g's—and the way she took an ordinary straight line for a "t" or "h" and made them look like calligraphy created in a beautiful note left by a woodland fairy. And I love all the colors she used! I can tell where her unique drawing style evolved into the beautiful stained glass windows she has restored and created for so many years.

Her first entry was written about Aidan on a background she had painted of the mountains east of our house. The horizon meets the mountains in a way that gives the most amazing yellow, orange and purple shades of light, which are often captured in the early morning hours as daylight begins to illuminate our orchard. The way Grandma used watercolors on this entry makes me feel like I am seeing a sunrise firsthand. I bet I know exactly where she was sitting. I make a note to myself to go out there today to see if I am right. For now, I need to focus on what she has to say...

Sophie's Journal
July—a hot summer night

Meant to Dance

Meet me on the mountainside
Where forever is just a moon away
Tell me however high we fly
That I am where you will stay
Listen to intuition and
Know nothing is by chance
Cradle my soul because you and I
Were meant to dance

I am such a silly, stupid girl. I don't know why I am suddenly intrigued by this kid Aidan. Just a couple of months ago, I barely knew who he was! Now I all I do is think about our night in the rain. I even wrote a silly poem called "Meant to Dance." "Cradle my soul..." who writes things like that????

I find him interesting. I hadn't realized he moved into the old Davidson farmhouse. I heard more about his older brothers from my sister Maggie Grace, MG as I like to call her. She apparently thinks one of them is her destiny. Disgusting. Disgusting because I don't want to think about my sister tongue- kissing some dude. Gross! Anyway...I guess he must of moved in when Mom, MG and I were stuck in the apartment downtown after the fire. Weird.

Now that we had that night, he keeps looking at me at school or in town when we happen to see one another as if he is going to say something, but never does. I can't help but stare back at his peculiar gazes and wonder what goes on behind those deep hazel-brown eyes. I think there must be a lot because he looks so serious. I wonder where he got that from. Whatever. I am just being stupid.

Sophie's Journal
Mid-July (still hot!)

I can't believe it, but Aidan told my friend Kat tonight that he likes me. We were all talking about going to the Lake tonight and he said to Kat that he had to talk to her. I felt a little jealous because I have started to really like spending time with Aidan. No one knows that we meet almost daily (day or night). I think we don't say anything because we aren't sure what it is we feel or even what this is. We don't kiss or try any moves on one another. We get so caught up in talking and laughing that even when I do think about kissing him, the moment passes so quickly that I actually forget!

I like it most when I can't sleep and wander out to the orchard's lawn late at night and find that Aidan is already out there, gazing up at the stars. We talk for hours about all sorts of things. Everything really. It is so cool. Anyway, Kat finally came back and told me that we had to hurry up and get ready to ride down to the lake on our bikes. Everyone was almost there. Peddling fast in the hot summer night, she said that Aidan wanted to know the best way to be my boyfriend! I almost peed myself giggling with excitement.

I asked her what she thought I should do. She turned back to look at me as her bike kept moving forward like I had three heads and told me how stupid it would be for me not to do (yet I am not the one riding a bike without looking where I am going). She said that Aidan was weird, but cool; perfect for me. I didn't take offense since most people referred to me as the "tree girl." It is a fair assumption that they think I am weird.

I knew tonight I would kiss Aidan in the lake under the Greenhill moon and I couldn't have been happier. AND THAT IS EXACTLY what we did!

Regardless of my mother's ideas about dating, I am not too young to have a boyfriend. I am fourteen now. Didn't Great-Grandma get married at fourteen? Or is that betrothed? Who knows what they did in Ireland. Who cares! Aidan and I are *meant to dance…* and that is exactly what I am going to do. I am officially "smitten," as one of my aunts likes to say. Oh, yes. Yes I am! Smitten with both feet in, face blushing when I talk about him and my heart pounding a thousand times just thinking about him!

Holy crap! I had no idea just how much Grandma had fallen for Aidan. I had never heard the full story and never had been given the impression that they had met so long ago. Dang. The women in this family never stop surprising me. Secrets. Secrets. Secrets...

I need to check on Grandma and see how she is doing with Aidan.

We had agreed that he would come early in the morning because knowing Sophie, she would be out of the house for one reason or another and he would miss her. I know they are going to need a lot of time together especially after all these years and all that has to be talked about. But I really want to keep reading...maybe just one more entry...

Sophie's Journal
July (two days after our first kiss)

I haven't been able to stop thinking about Aidan. It is ridiculous and I don't care! Mom was on my case this morning to check on the apple trees and clean up any branches that may have fallen in the last rain storm we had. She obviously figured out that I didn't do it the last time she told me, too.

Enough about my workaholic mother and back to Aidan. I was taking my time today wandering among the trees when I came to where Aidan and I usually meet. We have marked the spot with a ribbon tied to a limb that is not easily seen by anyone, of course, but us. Today, I found a note folded up and tucked in the elbow of our tree.

I felt like I would melt! Aidan was thinking of me! When I opened it, I read it slowly. Then I read it again and again and again. It simply said:

You haven't left my mind, not even for a second.

I think we are in love. Actually, I know I am. I danced and ran all the way back to the house. I couldn't stop smiling and I couldn't wait to see him again. I raced up the stairs to my room and pulled out my secret hiding box. I carefully placed my first note from Aidan on top of the first flowers we picked together and gathered myself enough to head back out to the orchard before my mother had a fit! And believe me she would have had I not run right back out.

But another great thing happened!!!!! Aidan was in the orchard waiting for me. He asked me if I had found something in the tree for me. I ran over to him and gave him a huge hug. We kissed and kissed. I don't know how I ever pulled myself back together to start gathering up broken branches but thank god I did. It actually went by fast because Aidan helped.

After I convinced my mother to let me go swimming with Aidan and my friends I had the best day in my entire life. I had soooo much fun! I think Aidan did, too.

I don't know what to think after reading Grandma Sophie's journal. Initially, I was very excited to learn where their story began, but now I have more questions than answers. It is not what I expected. First, I didn't know that she even had journals from when she was that young. I was really looking for the part when she and Aidan broke up. Why did they do that? How did they know that was right for them? But Grandma Sophie always has a reason for what she says and does and I know she pointed me to this journal at this time for an important message.

As for now, the only thing that comes to me is my own journal about when Dan and I first started dating and how much I can relate to how Sophie felt toward Aidan. Maybe it is an age thing, given that Dan and I started dating around the same age as Sophie and Aiden.

The only other thought that comes to mind is how much she has indicated her belief in Dan and I having a great life together. She has only vaguely once hinted that she thought Dan and I were like her and Aidan. The way she looks at us has always told me that. When I see large tears well up in her eyes, and her efforts to push them away, I sense her joy, as well as deep sorrow. I never really understood it and never asked. I always gave her a hug and thanked her for supporting us. Now, from what I have started to read today and Aidan wanting to make some sort of amends, I realize that discovering my own answers could possibly give Grandma some peace.

There is clearly a lot more to their story than I could have imagined and I am just going to have to keep reading. Gazing out the window that overlooks the path leading to their tree, I decide this is exactly the right time to check in with Sophie and Aidan. Maybe they can give me the "cliff note" version of their story. I doubt it, though. Sophie has rarely if ever answered my questions about life and love with a direct answer.

What I do know is that there has to be a very good reason she still cries sometimes when she comes back from the orchard.

11 a.m.

Aidan

*H*olding Sophie early this morning felt like I had finally come home. Gently taking her lovely face into my hands so I could kiss her and tell her how much I loved her, missed her, was more than I could hope for. Sophie stirs my soul in a way that makes me want to be more, say more, feel more. The electricity between us has always been palpable. We spent so much time talking and being together this morning I have barely had time to catch my breath. I am so grateful.

Had I not made a quick run to pick up some basic groceries at the Greenhill General Store a few months back, when I was preparing the house for my permanent return to Greenhill, I would have never had learned about Sophie's granddaughter, Jori. I would most likely not be talking about the bundle of nerves I felt today arriving back up on the Hill to see Sophie.

Fortunately, that is one of the benefits of a small town. Rarely is it difficult to find out what you have missed over the decades you might have been gone. With just a brief conversation at the General Store, you can essentially find out a myriad of things. Everything from who married whom, who had babies, who died. I have loved and hated that.

Many years have passed and now I am in my nineties, as she is. If I have a chance to make things right with her, I know this would most likely be my very last opportunity to do so. I admit, there were times when I wondered if she was still alive.

There is too much I have to say to her and too much at stake. I am never going to walk away from her again. Not ever. I have to let her know that, even if she walks away from me.

As if the Universe had heard my struggle, while I was at the store, a lovely young woman walked in, the unmistakable glow of pregnancy radiating from her. Several hellos were exchanged between her and the other patrons. I was stunned by her incredible similarity to Sophie. Jori's hair was slightly darker, but she had the same light in her eyes and her whole demeanor immediately washed away any concerns I had about approaching her to introduce myself.

Admittedly, I was pleasantly surprised by Jori's friendly response when I presented her with my idea of visiting her grandmother on The Hill.

It turned out that not only had Jori heard of me because my family's home was on the other side of the eastern tree line, but she knew that Sophie had been with me many years ago. I was even more surprised when she began laughing about my insecurity with regard to Sophie. Seeing the look of confusion on my face, she gathered herself enough to elaborate.

"Aidan, I am sure Grandma would love to see you! I can't believe after all this time, you would think that she wouldn't. You were always different for her and so young when everything happened between you two. She may be tough, but not that tough. I have lived with her my entire life and I think I am pretty good at knowing what would upset Grandma or not."

I paused to think about what she just said. I was not entirely certain that Jori could possibly understand my deep concern about seeing Sophie. This wasn't just about love lost; it was about making amends to someone with whom I had once thought I would spend the rest of my life.

This young woman couldn't possibly understand how much of my life I have spent feeling guilty and foolish, and wondering what my life could have been with Sophie.

"Well, the last time I saw your grandmother, I knew what I had lost. I walked away, but have never stopped looking back."

With a deep sigh and in a mournful tone, I continued to explain to Jori how much each of us made assumptions about what we felt for one another. How this is part of the reason we never created a life together.

"Our timing was always off after we broke up in college. We tried a couple of times to reconnect, just to catch up, but it never worked out well. In fact, the last time we saw one another, I realized without a doubt that she had moved on. I found out she had married your grandfather and had a baby, your father. In fact, I saw Sophie and the toddler playing together at Willow Lake one year when I came back to visit Greenhill."

Jori seemed willing to listen and was so easy to confide in. It has always been that way with the O'Neill women—they have a way of putting a person at ease. So I went on. "I had reached my thirties by then and had become successful in my own right, just as I said I would. I was engaged to be married to a really great woman and by all standards, I was on the right path. In fact, I had brought my fiancée with me. We were trying to decide if we should get married where I had grown up or in my fiancée's home town. It was looking like Greenhill would be that spot until I saw Sophie."

Gently, I guided Jori over to a bench against the wall. With her eyes, she encouraged me to continue.

"Despite my life being everything I said I wanted it to be and then some, I remember feeling more lonely than I had ever thought I could. It made no sense until I saw Sophie laughing and dancing around with your father that day on the water's edge. Spraying each other with water, as they kicked up their feet and threw sand pies at one another. I saw that same light in her. "

"When I saw Sophie that day, I could hardly breathe. I was crushed completely and I realized that it was my own damned fault. I had pushed her away to pursue my dreams and ideas of a life I wanted. I didn't genuinely take into account her feelings and dreams. I assumed we would figure it out and it would be fine.

"We didn't and she had to move on. Seeing her actually doing it was difficult. Far more for me so than I had imagined it would be. That is when I started having to face some of the lies I had been telling myself.

"Those lies came falling all around me that day I saw her on the beach. That night, I was confronted with the biggest one of all. I was trying to create a life with another woman I wanted to be Sophie. It wasn't fair.

"After an argument about how many people we thought we should invite and where we would get married… I realized I really didn't care. Not as much as I should have. It was my distance and my lack of interest that finally ended my engagement. After four years of being together, she had enough of it."

Jori looked at me with her big chocolate-brown eyes swimming with tears. "I had no idea, Aidan, and I don't think Sophie ever knew that, either. So you never got married? Had kids?"

"No, I didn't. I never let go of Sophie enough to feel I could, and I never let her know how I felt, so I wasn't able to commit either way. That's not to say I didn't try to change that. I had a couple of long-term relationships and they were great, but no one ever made me want to have that life enough. It never felt like home the way it did with Sophie. Sounds really pathetic, doesn't it, but it was what it was. I don't totally regret my choices, I only regret not letting Sophie know how sorry I was for pushing her away."

Jori reached out her slender hand and said, "That was so long ago, Aidan. I am not even sure she remembers that now. She never mentioned anything like that to me, but she has also had memory issues for many years from an awful car accident. Maybe that is why I haven't heard many details about what actually occurred between the two of you. Not sure. I guess there is only one way to find out. Right?"

So Jori and I made a plan for me to visit The Hill to see Sophie. There were a few things I had to wrap up in Washington before I could return to Greenhill permanently.

* * * * *

*T*he months passed in a painfully slow fashion and I must have second-guessed myself more than a hundred times or so. Thankfully, Jori and I began to exchange letters and she continued to assure me that Sophie would be thrilled to see me. I could also tell that Jori had the same determined streak in her possessed by all the O'Neill women I had encountered, so the likelihood of my backing out was virtually pointless.

Having this opportunity was more than I could have imagined or hoped for. All this time, I felt that Sophie hated me. The last time we had seen each other felt like a lifetime ago. It broke my heart in a way I didn't know possible. I blamed myself for so long that I never allowed for the idea that Sophie had forgiven me for being me. I had been young and foolish. There is was no way to know what course our lives would have taken otherwise.

Now here I am, an old man. Hoping to capture some forgiveness from a person who by all standards had no obligation to afford me the time of day. I am humbled and tired from the years of building homes for others. Hands scarred from more injuries than I can count and a body that aches with each step I take—the consequence of countless decades of working year round in whatever weather the Northwest or New England tossed at me.

I have amassed a small fortune building homes for folks who had become bored with the city life and thought that by having a multi-million-dollar house in the country, they could salvage their souls. The souls they left in the city to pay for all the fancy cars, trips, clothes, and so forth. In a way, I had sold a part of me, too. I was rewarded financially doing what I did and I was good.

In an effort to take that guilt of being a "sell-out," like Sophie said I would become, and placing it neatly on a shelf somewhere in the deep recesses of my mind, each year I would anonymously build five homes for families in Greenhill and the surrounding towns who had lost their homes due to financial strain, fire, or some sort of natural disaster. It was a great way to keep my guilty conscious at bay by taking the time to create a home for those who had dreams of leaving a legacy for their children and the many generations to come.

This worked for a long time and bought me more nights of sleep than I would have gotten otherwise. It wasn't until I retired and I stopped working seventy-plus hours a week that it hit me like a ton of bricks.

Sophie was right. They were the same people Sophie used to talk about—the people who made her so angry because picking apples was somehow correlated with IQ and life potential. Anyone could grow and pick apples, right? Anyone could build houses, right? I was just a New England boy who had grown up to become an architect, but never let go of his hands-on, down-to-earth carpenter's roots. I worked twice as hard to push away the dissonance within me and built an impeccable reputation.

In my retirement, I found myself literally alone and had nothing but time and money. Nothing but myself to look at in the mirror, knowing my time on earth was quickly coming to an end.

* * * * *

I had been up most of the night anticipating seeing Sophie again. By the time I arrived at her house early this morning, I was operating on pure adrenaline comprised of nerves and lack of sleep. It had only been a few days since I had been able to catch a glimpse of her by the apple trees, which I thought would have helped me prepare more when I went to see her today, but I still felt anxious.

There was no way I was turning back, regardless of how tight and nauseated my stomach felt. I had firmly decided that after having been able to see her this closely after all these years, I would no longer hesitate or make excuses as to why I should not go to her.

I knew that early morning would be the best time to see her. I didn't want to take a chance of her leaving to do an errand or to go one of her walks and not be able to see her right away.

It was so wonderful to catch a glimpse of her walking where we had spent so much time talking, playing, and dreaming as kids. I am almost certain that by the time I had seen her on the lawn the other day, she had found her spot on the grass, nestled amongst the apple trees where it was just right for her to sit or lie down. She loved taking naps in the warmth of the midday sun or falling asleep under the stars at night. She would sing, write and draw until she had to go inside.

Not a bit of that seems to have changed over the time I have spent away from her; I am so grateful for that. It means that no matter what has come in or out of Sophie's life, she has never lost who she is and what she has passion for. And she is just a beautiful as I remember. I have never met anyone who loved being outside as much as Sophie. She used to tell me how she could feel the ground breathe beneath her and hear the trees whisper secrets of all that they have seen.

It always felt like an honor that she was willing to share her world with me. She held this place so deeply within her that when we made some of it ours. I knew I would never feel more at home. Eventually, I came to feel the ground breathe and the trees whisper their secrets to me, too. But I am not sure my connection was ever as deep as hers.

Being outside was an extension of her self. It was a seamless transition whenever she entered outdoor space, as if she somehow magnified the sights and sounds that most of us barely noticed. Sophie brought the outside world in and the inside world out.

It's hard to comprehend that a simple trip to the store would give me an opportunity I thought I would never have again.

In the quiet moments today, I replayed how our story began. Some might say that I was doing a relationship review, but for me, it marked a review of a lifetime—my lifetime and what I have to come to know about myself.

The first time I saw Sophie, she was walking down Main Street in our town of Greenhill. She was smiling and laughing with a friend. Kat was other girl's name, I think. There was a lightness about Sophie that instantly drew me to her. It wasn't love at first sight, more like an intense curiosity about what made her laugh the way she did. It was genuine, deep joy I heard. Spontaneous and expressed so completely with each giggle that it became deeper and longer each time it found its way to my ears.

The second time we met was at what became "our tree," standing under the moonlight, getting soaked by the rain, on one of the many grassy paths between the gnarled apple trees in the O'Neill orchard.

* * * * *

I was lying in my bed on a hot, summer evening with my windows open so I could listen to the rain fall. It was such a relief after the long, muggy, humid day we had. I had grown very annoyed by the humming of fans all day and welcomed the natural sound of cooling down.

New England can be brutally hot in the summer. With all the trees and densely wooded areas, it makes you feel like you are a wet towel on a ninety-degree day. You just feel rubbery and almost weak with fatigue from the intensity of the heat and moisture. No fan or lack of clothing could take away that feeling completely. Surrendering was all any of us could do until the rain would come and bring a slight chill to the air.

Now that the rain was beginning to cut the humidity, my restlessness forced me to get up. I looked out at the neighbor's apple trees and thought I saw someone moving around. Dancing around even. I was bored, possibly delusional, from staring at my rotating ceiling fan for so long. I wanted to know if I what I thought I was seeing was actually true. Besides, I was fourteen, and constantly seeking something new and exciting to do, because, let's face it—Greenhill was not exactly hopping with activity. So I jumped up and walked outside in the rain wearing just a t-shirt and shorts.

As I began walking toward whoever or whatever was out there, I could hear a soft voice singing. Trying to place the tune, I realized I had no idea what the song was and in a matter of seconds, saw that it was Sophie O'Neill. Even on that dark, rainy night, I had that same curiosity about her. The same lightness came with each word she sang and each time she hummed.

Not wanting to scare her, I cleared my throat and said, "Hey! Whatcha doing out here?"

"I am dancing. What does it look like?"

"Yes, well I can see that and hear you singing, too. But why in the rain? Seems kind of weird."

With a small giggle, she came running over to me and grabbed both my hands and before I realized what was happening, I was dancing, too! The more we spun and twirled, I found myself laughing in a way I hadn't for a very long time. I knew then that it was the same sort of laughter I had heard in Sophie. I began to let myself feel joy; I couldn't stop laughing and dancing. I didn't want to.

My intense nature was loosening its grip on me. It felt so good. I felt lighter in my steps, less gloomy and negative about the events that had been going on in my life. All I know is that it felt great! I never wanted to leave that warm summer rain, her laughter and her light. Never.

I closed my eyes and with my arms stretched up toward the sky above me, I felt myself let go. Let go of my worries, the brooding I had done since moving to the house near the orchard, and my anger for my life not going the way I thought it should go.

When I opened my eyes again, Sophie was gone.

I recall standing there, waiting for some sort of movement from her or the sound of her laughter, singing—anything! But there was nothing but the sound of the rain beating down on the leaves and grassy earth. Suddenly I felt cold and began shivering. I ran back into my house and dried myself off. That night, I fell asleep with so many thoughts and questions in my head. But only one I came back to: *When will I ever get to see her again?*

After that night in the rain, I began to go outside at night to see if I could catch a glimpse of her or maybe hear her hum some strange tune. After a few days, I decided to just sit go and by a tree. Walking around started to make me feel like a stalker. Of course, that wasn't the case, but I was cognizant of the fact that this was her family's property and not so sure I should be walking around on it as it pleased me. Fortunately, it was a particularly bright evening because of the moon and I felt confident I would be able to see her should she be out tonight.

I decided to lie down on the soft grass and look up at the stars. God, it was beautiful! No wonder she seemed to love being out here.

Suddenly, I heard a soft swooshing sound. When I looked up, I could see her coming toward me. The first thought that came to my mind was, *Now what, idiot!?* I had been so focused on seeing her that I hadn't thought about what I might actually say to her if I encountered her again.

"Hey, Aidan! Glad you came back. I knew you would. You seemed so happy in the rain."

Practically stuttering, I answered awkwardly, "Glad to be here."

"Well, that's fantastic that we are both glad."

"I can see why you love it out here, Sophie. It is so incredibly beautiful. I can't believe I never thought of coming out here before."

"Me, either. No one would have cared if you had. Although I don't think my mother would have taken it too well if you started to pick our apples. We sell those apples to help cover our winter expenses. Tourists think it is fun to pick them and buy up all the baked goods we make. And don't even get me started about our apple chutney! They freak out about it! Sort of lame, but it gets us what we need."

"Sounds smart to me. But what do I know, right?"

Laughing, she said, "Oh, you're right. It is smart. I just get an attitude (according to my mother) when I have to work extra in the fall. And I don't like the way rich people talk to us like we are stupid or something."

"Yeah, I get ya. Sometimes I get irritated by the tourists, too, but what would Greenhill be like if they didn't come?" I asked.

"Well, it's completely annoying that you just made sense."

"I know, I am kind of good at that—you know, annoying people."

We both smiled and allowed it to get quiet.

That night, we spent hours together. Talking, laughing, sharing more than I ever knew you could with a girl. Most of my friends were focused on making out with girls, not talking about music, hobbies, or dreams of a future outside of Greenhill. I'm not saying I didn't think about kissing Sophie. I definitely did. It was just that we got caught up in simply hanging out and getting to know one another. I quickly felt I had found a new best friend.

How the hell was I going to explain this to my buddies? *Yah...so you see...there is this girl I love to be with, but uh, I don't really want to do it with her...get it?* I could just feel their stares bore into me, then their roars of laughter, questions about how ugly she was. After I explained that I thought she was the most beautiful girl I had ever seen, I would then be accused of being gay and reminded that there were a lot of other "hot babes out there." That I shouldn't get so serious especially over one girl.

But none of that mattered when I was with Sophie. I didn't care. I would figure it out. The time with her was too important to me to get caught up in all that crap.

That night marked just one of many Sophie and I would meet up on the grass beneath the apple trees. "*Our tree*" is what it became on an unspoken level. Sometimes we hung out during the day, which became easier as our parents started to grow suspicious by the frequency we kept asking to go out for walks at night. I think they mostly thought we were trying to smoke pot or drink, neither of which interested us when we were together.

We learned that we actually had been living across the orchard from one another for a few months. Hard to believe but we never knew who it was we would see at the edge of the trees that separated our houses until, of course, that night in the rain.

I always thought she was interesting and never got enough of looking at her beautiful, chocolate-brown eyes and her light, golden-brown hair. She was sweet and weird and funny as hell. It was easy to amuse her, too. It was like there was nothing she couldn't find interesting or positive. She was always drawing and listening to music I had never heard of. I loved every sweet moment we got to hang out at the tree, our tree.

Part Two

Afternoon

Sophie

D rifting between a dream and recollections about my morning, I am jolted fully back to the present with a door shutting loudly and Jori calling my name. What time is it? Afternoon? Evening? I feel so tired. Last thing I remember, I was talking with Aidan about Jori and Dan and wondering if there was anything we could do to help them not make the mistakes we did.

Looking around, I try to gain a sense of time. I can't find my watch. Damn. Probably left that somewhere, too. I smell a turkey roasting and the homemade bread I had enjoyed earlier this morning with Aidan and Jori. The wonderful aroma has flooded the house and I am instantly hungry as I envision eating more warm bread with butter and some of our apple chutney on it. I could that eat every day.

I slowly get up to stretch and my bones naturally adjust as I start looking around the house. Where is Jori? Where is Aidan? It upsets me greatly that I remember less and less each day. I don't understand how I can lose track of time, but they say that happens in old age. I reassure myself that this habit of mine is natural. I am older, therefore I need more sleep. Naps are frequent for me and when I sit in the library drinking my tea, it is practically guaranteed that I will drift asleep. Which is exactly what happened this morning.

"Jori," I call out. "I am up now. Where are you?"

I listen for her to call back, but instead I hear a man's voice talking. Must be Dan. I walk through the kitchen and toward the front entrance and see Jori talking to him. I can see she has been crying and they are hugging. *Maybe*, I think to myself, *they are figuring this out.*

"Hey, Dan!" I call out. "Great to see you."

"Great to see you, too, Sophie. I hear Aidan is here."

"He is indeed. But I don't know where he is now. Do you know, Jori?"

"Oh, yeah, he said he was going to pick up a few things from town and then stop by his folks' place to see his brother and kids. We weren't sure when you would be up, but I expect he will be back any time now. I can't wait for you to meet him, Dan. I have had such a great morning with Grandma and Aidan. I think you are really going to enjoy spending time with them, too."

"Absolutely. I can't wait. Hey, listen, can I get more stuff from my car, Jori? I want to get settled back in before Aidan gets back. Then I'd like to hear all about these two."

"Sure, of course. I'll help. I will be right back, Sophie."

Watching them walk hand in hand to Dan's car makes me feel hopeful. Jori is beginning to understand how important it is to look at a situation differently. Without your pride. Without your fear to cloud your judgment and interfere with what is meant to be. I love watching their dance, but it is hard to see them struggle so unnecessarily.

Well, I suppose that is a bit ironic, isn't it? Standing back and looking at a situation is quite different than when you feel like you are drowning in one. I suspect my mother and those closest to me felt similarly when Aidan and I were together and of course, when I was with Ollie's father, too.

"I'm back!" Aidan calls out, suddenly appearing with Jori and Dan practically on his heels as he steps through the doorway. He immediately hugs me and apologizes for being longer than he thought he would.

"No problem, Aidan. I just woke up for the second time today," I laugh.

Seeing him standing in the foyer again after all these years feels surreal. I had imagined this reunion so many times, for so many years, that it is practically indescribable now that it is happening. I happily begin to replay the moment I saw him standing in that very spot early this morning.

* * * * *

I had gone outside briefly to smell the air at dawn to see if I could determine my plan for the day. It's something I have done on a regular basis whenever I think rain or snow is on the way. It works, so I have never tried anything different. I never rely on the weather reports. They somehow always seem to get the timing of weather conditions wrong.

When I came back inside, I called out to Jori, but got no response, so I began looking for her. When I found her,

I saw that she was talking to an older man in the doorway. What the heck? I looked at the wooden clock, set against the wall next to my cardinal painting and saw it was still early. I am confused. I can't help but wonder who would be coming here this early?

"Jori? What's going on? Who's there?" I asked, uncertainty fluttering in my breast.

"Oh, Grandma, there you are! I was about to get you. She turned toward me and motioned me to hurry to the door. "Come here, come here. I have a great surprise for you."

I approached the entrance way and felt my body getting warmer and my stomach started doing flip-flops. My hands and arms started to shake. Is that who I think it is? How is that possible?

As I walked closer to the doorway, I was completely overcome with a feeling of familiarity and I felt my body go slightly numb. It was Aidan. Here! Now!

In my shock, I simply stared at his face. There, beneath the signs of hard work and age, I saw the young man I had fallen in love at age fourteen. The same deep hazel brown eyes. I was in awe and placed my hands on my heart to steady its rapid beating as I allowed the well of tears slide down my cheeks. I was in absolute disbelief that he was standing here. Really here.

"Sophie?" he asked slowly and cautiously.

I couldn't say anything in response. Only hear my inner dialogue that said over and over... "He is here. He is here. He came back. He really came back!"

Despite Jori's telling me that he had contacted her and he wanted to see me, it had been months ago (I think). I had agreed, of course, but there was a part of me that didn't believe that it would actually happen. But there he was! Really, really there. Happiness flooded through me.

I still couldn't find the words. All I wanted to do was hold him. I just wanted to hug him and feel his arms around me. I closed my eyes, hoping it was not some imagined version of how I had dreamed this moment would be and how it would feel.

Before I knew it, I felt his arms wrap around me and despite the trembling I felt throughout my body, I was able to hug him back. This was very real and very much like I had imagined doing hundreds of times since we broke up when we were nineteen.

I felt like it was just yesterday that we had embraced one another beneath our tree. I felt his body begin to shake as he sobbed, holding me close to him. I still fit in the base of his neck and he still had the same smell I remember. The smell of pine and fresh air.

Holding him and being held was wonderful. I was consumed with the comfort I felt with him. How loved I was in that moment. I couldn't help but sob, too, realizing how much I missed this feeling. This feeling of being home, of being so loved by a man. This man.

This is what I hoped for, lost, and mourned. My time with Aidan had such a deep impact on my life and ultimately guided me to who I became. He brought out the very best in me and the kindness and love he gave me never left me, not even in my darkest moments. His love was what helped me through a point in my life when I thought so little of myself that I didn't care if I lived or died, the dire consequence of having stayed with Ollie's father for the years I did.

Of course, at the time, I didn't realize just how severe a toll that relationship took on my spirit—until I almost got my wish to permanently leave this world behind. It was a severe, but necessary, wake-up call for me to begin living fully again.

I sobbed with gratitude that he had come to me after all this time. I sobbed for time lost and this chance to ensure Aidan knows how sorry I was for whatever I did that may have hurt him. Especially when we last parted. It is a horrible thing to carry over the years—having lashed out at another in a moment of hurt and later realizing that was the last impression that person was given of you. It has gnawed at me for so long that I had been cruel and had said mean things to him.

I think that is one of the reasons I stayed so long with Ollie's father—it was payback for how I had treated Aidan when we broke up. Eventually, I came to realize that a moment of anger did not justify the years of abuse I had endured with Ollie's father. I just prayed that Aidan was able to remember the best of what I had given him and not the last shameful moments we had together.

For the second time today and after several moments in each other's arms, Aiden and I finally pulled apart and looked into one another's eyes. Wiping our tears away, we linked our arms together and walked further into the foyer, where Jori was crying, too.

"Oh, this is exactly how I imagined you two seeing one another again. It's so beautiful," she said.

Aidan and I looked at each other and laughed.

"Jori, you have read waaay too many romance novels," I said playfully.

"Very true, Grandma, but no story has felt like this."

"Well, you haven't heard all of it yet, dear. Not sure what you will think when you do," I said kindly.

"I can't imagine it will change my mind about what I see right now. It will probably make it that much sweeter," Jori said.

"Perhaps, but for now, let's go to the library and enjoy this. I can't stop shaking and I need to sit."

"Great idea, Sophie. I can't stop shaking either," Aidan said, smiling. "You know, Jori, the library was our favorite place to be together in this house."

"I can't believe you remember that, Aidan!" I said with amazement.

"I certainly do. It was a wonderful, comfortable place. There is so much I remember about being here, being with you. I don't know how to adequately tell you how excited I am to be back here on The Hill, in this house, and with you, Sophie. After we broke up, I rarely went back to my folks' house."

Aiden continued, "I couldn't bear the thought of running into you and trying to figure out what to do. Thankfully, Mom let one of my brothers take it over so she could manage a small place of her own. After my parents divorced and Dad left, it wasn't so bad for her when I was still around. Once I went away, though, it was very hard for her to keep up the property. To be completely honest, I don't think she wanted to. She had only held onto it for me. As soon as she realized I wanted her to be happy, she gifted the house to my brother and his family. Dad certainly didn't care, so it became a win-win situation for everyone.

"At the time, I thought it was great timing, but knowing now what I do, I can see it only hurt me. After I stopped finding ways to make sure I didn't have to face you again, Sophie, I began to hope that I would have this kind of chance again. To say I am an idiot is an understatement."

* * * * *

I can't seem to find the words to respond to Aidan as dozens of thoughts and questions speed through my mind. I had never imagined he thought about me much after we broke up and began our lives without one another. I guess it made it easier to think that so I could find a way to let him go.

The silence in the small library begins to feel heavy and I am grateful to hear Jori say, "Okay, I will meet you both back here in the library after I check the bread and turkey. Would either of you like some tea?"

"That would be great, Jori, thanks. You are so sweet," I say with a smile.

"Wait! Do you still have your apple chutney? I would love some if you have it," Aidan says.

"Of course we have it, Aidan! Good Lord, do you think we would still be here on The Hill without our chutney?" I laugh heartily.

"What was I thinking? Of course, you wouldn't," Aidan says with a playful wink. "Sophie, you are so beautiful and lovely—just as I imagined you would be if either of us got to this age."

"Thank you, Aidan. I was thinking something similar about you. In fact, the reason I kept staring at you is because I was astounded at how much I could still see that young man I met dancing in the rain."

"Is this really happening, Sophie? Are we really sitting here in your library and holding hands and smiling like it was just yesterday that we met and fell in love?

Jori walks back in with tea, homemade bread, butter, and the O'Neil chutney.

"What did I miss?" Jori asks eagerly.

"Nothing really. Just enjoying one another's company."

"You betcha. Now where is that chutney?" Aidan reaches over to take the dish from Jori.

I can't help but smile and don't remember feeling such joy in years.

2 p.m.

Jori

"So that's pretty much how my day has been, Dan. Seeing those two reconnect was amazing and I feel honored to have been a part of it."

"Well, we are glad you helped out, Jori," Aidan says.

"Yes, thank God. I am not sure what would have happened if you hadn't been so willing to help Aidan when he asked, Jori." Sophie takes Aidan's hand again and holds it to her heart. "I am so happy to feel this love with you again, Aidan. So, so happy you took a chance on me."

"I had to, Sophie. I absolutely had to. I wasted so much of my life being afraid to do what I did this morning and now here we are, in our nineties and getting to talk, laugh, and hold each other. Please know that I never did stop thinking of you, Sophie. Nor did I ever stop loving you. I simply made myself manage without you and it is a deep regret." Aidan gets teary again and Sophie strokes his hand to comfort him.

"It's okay, Aidan. I did the same. I also managed to live my life without you, but truly, never stopped loving you. I used to get so angry with myself when I thought of you and I wondered what was wrong with me. Why didn't I just let you go?"

"Um, speaking of letting go, why did you guys break up? What happened?" Dan asks.

"Dan! I can't believe you just said that to them. My goodness! They haven't seen each other forever and you want them to tell us why they broke up?!" I say in a teasing tone.

Jumping to Dan's defense, Sophie looks at me a little sternly. "Oh, give him a break, Jori. He asked a great question. If I were sitting where he is, I would be asking the same question. Since when did any of us in this family hold our tongue when we thought something? I suppose there is still a lot for Aidan and me to talk about today, and when we get to that place, we will do our best to share it with you."

"You're right, Grandma. I'm sorry, Dan," I reach over to give him a kiss and hug and sigh, "I am ridiculous sometimes, I know. It's that O'Neill in me."

"Sweetheart, don't worry so much about offending me. We have been around one another way too long for you to worry about that. I know your heart. I really do. I always appreciate your intentions—just not your delivery sometimes," Dan chuckles.

I then turn to Sophie and say, "When I was reading your journal this morning, Sophie, I couldn't imagine you and Aidan ending up here. All this time having gone by without one another."

Looking at each other, Sophie and Aidan sigh in unison. "I guess it was just our dance, Jori," Sophie says quietly. "I know Aidan and I need to tell you more of our story and we will, but I think maybe you should try reading more of my journals to see if you can capture what was felt at the time. Not just what we recollect now. Things change,

Jori, and perspectives shift. I am not sure hearing us describe our story today would have the same impact as reading about it when it was actually happening. Does that make sense?"

"I think so, Grandma. Would you mind if Dan came upstairs with me?"

"Of course not, Jori. I think that is a great idea. If Dan wants to, of course."

"Yes, I would really like that, but I can't believe you would be so open and share your innermost thoughts with me, Sophie," Dan says, almost shyly.

"Dan, you are family and always will be. If it can help you and Jori find your way back to one another in a way that assures you both that what you have is very real and worth holding onto, then I am going to try it. Besides I am too old to give a darn about what you might think of me, good or bad. I figure it will either help you or it won't, but I am betting on it helping."

"Thanks, Grandma." I take Dan's hand and we walk upstairs to the baby's room. I hear Sophie and Aidan talking in soft voices and then music coming from the old record player downstairs. As much as I think Grandma wants to help me and Dan, I also think she and Aidan want to simply spend some time together, without us. It must be so magical to feel what they feel after all these years and to know that it wasn't ever a question of not loving one another.

As I lift the lid to Gratia's steamer trunk, I wonder which journal I should pick next. Let's see, I kept the one Sophie guided me to this morning on top of the dresser, so I will check to see when her entries stopped and hopefully with Dan's help, we can find the next one.

Pointing to the stack of journals, I say, "Hey, Dan, can you look through these starting sometime at the end of July beginning of August? It would have been when she was around fourteen. Usually she writes her age on the first page each time she started a new journal."

"No problem. I already started sorting what look to be older journals from Sophie's mother and grandmothers. I don't want to mess with those and break them or something. They look pretty old and sort of frail."

"Great point. Thanks for thinking of that, Jori."

I walk back over to Dan and I see where he has separated out the journals. There seem to be dozens from the women in my family, so it has taken longer than we thought it would. But having gotten those organized into separate piles, Dan and I begin flipping to the first page of Sophie's journals, working our way from the top to the bottom of the pile.

After going through at least a half of dozen of them, Dan excitedly says to me, "Look at this, Jori! I think this is it! See the picture on the front? It is different from all the others. There also seem to be two others just like it."

Reaching out to take the journal from Dan, I instantly see what he means. Of course! I know this picture. It is the same design from the window that Sophie had installed during my dad's renovation on the house. She was very particular about it, micromanaging the care and the placement of it when Dad started to re-design some parts of the family home.

* * * * *

Sitting back in the rocker, I reflect.

We all thought she was being picky because, for one, she is old and set in her ways. Second, when she gets her mind set on something, it has to be done, regardless if in the future she changes her mind, often doing what we initially suggested to her. Last but not least, because it was the only piece she ever designed and completed that she actually kept for herself.

Over the years, most her pieces of stained glass art have been sold, donated, or given away as gifts. She never kept her completed pieces, even though there were times I could tell it was very hard for her to part with them. Each one carried a bit of her in it and she often spent weeks, even months, working on a piece. I can only imagine how hard it is to let something go like that, something you spent so many hours creating and getting to know so intimately, each delicate piece carefully selected and positioned.

For Grandma, each piece has a story. For example, the time she created the window for the general store in town. It took her months to design because she wanted it to be perfect. It had to be something that everyone could relate to, whether a person was new to town or had been here for generations like we had. She agonized until finally at 3 a.m. one morning, she began the construction of the window that now sits above the entry way to the store.

Sophie didn't just design a piece with its colors in mind or how big or small it had to be; she also took into account the lighting at different times of the day and how the glass she chose showed each person who looked at it that it was special in its own right. She didn't just want people to stop in awe at how beautiful the window was; she also wanted them to connect with it on a personal level. That somehow, her art moved each viewer, so that whatever building it was displayed in, people would feel a positive connection to that place as well.

Some said she was way too intense about her work, but I have yet to meet an artist who wasn't. It is what makes Sophie who she is and what she gives us visually and personally. If her glass designs stirs happiness in a person, she feels successful. I suspect her passion for doing such pieces had to do with her lifelong pursuit to be happy herself. I think she figured that if she could help others feel that way, that eventually she would be able to do that for herself again.

Great-Aunt Maggie Grace and Dad both said she was never the same after being with my grandfather. I never got the full story, only that he passed away suddenly and Sophie went into a very deep depression. Only her art and being on The Hill saved her. She needed both and fortunately, she had them.

I am so glad she found her way out of that darkness. I couldn't imagine my life without her. It saddens me so much to think that my grandmother thought so little of herself at one point. She is the most amazing, strong and interesting person I have ever met.

Running my hands over the picture so carefully sealed on the outside of the journal, I am sure that this is the one that will pick up where the other left off. I have a feeling with these next few journals, Dan and I are going to learn something. Something really important.

Settling in on the small sofa in the baby's room, Dan and I carefully open the journal and begin reading, taking in the background of painted green and purple trees on the page Sophie began her entry.

Sophie's Journal
(Still 14 but almost 15yrs. old)

Life cannot feel any more perfect! Summer is still here and I cannot imagine being more happy than I am now. Ever! Ever! Aidan and I are doing great! We finally told our friends that we are together (although many of them already knew) and somehow this seems to make us more in love. I guess we just want everyone to know how much we care for each other…or something like that. Even my mother likes him! That is enough to shock everyone.

Well, as much as I could babble on about how much I love Aidan and being with him, I am going to go. Don't really feel like writing as much as I do drawing. I have a design in mind and I don't want to let it slip from my mind.

Turning the page, Dan and I see Sophie's very first design of the window she so heavily guarded during the renovation. Its lovely colors create a stunning view of the orchard and cast rainbows against the wall when the sun hits it just right. She said she wanted the first morning sun to shine through it, so the stained glass window had to be placed on the eastern wall so she could see it each day when the sun came up.

I look at the faint pencil outline of a tree—probably an apple tree—with the mountains as a backdrop. She has marked what colors she is considering for each part of her sketch. Turning to see if there are more drafts, I am not disappointed. There are her second and third drawings, now done with beautiful purple, white, and green mountains. The central image of the tree seems to have come to life with a light blue and silver glow surrounding its branches and leaves. It is beautiful.

There is only one other draft. In it, she has added two birds, but had not yet colored like the other parts of her picture. The next page is torn out and I recognize the jagged edges of the picture placed on the front of the journal. Sophie had placed her original on the outside.

I close my eyes and ask, "Sophie, what do I need to know? What am I missing?"

Sophie's Journal
September
(Still 14 but Aidan is now 15
and fall is coming very soon)

We celebrated Aidan's birthday at the house and then with our friends. His mom came over and seems to fit in quite well with the rest of the lunatics in my family. This is a good thing. If this was not the case then Aidan and I were surely doomed. Doomed, doomed. Know what I mean?

I will turn 15 within the next few months, so Aidan and I are practically the same age.

Dan and I keep reading about the many days and months Aidan and Sophie spent together. Through entries about the changing seasons and special events like birthdays, holidays and O'Neill gatherings. Before we know it, we have followed Sophie and Aidan through the years of their dance.

I am in love with them. I am in love with their story. With each entry, I am pulled deeper into their dance. The pictures and entries I read only confirm how much they truly loved one another.

One of my favorites is a page that Sophie draws of a "snow cave" that Aidan built for them. I can see how much he thought of her and how much magic they created together...

Sophie's Journal
(February and it is VERY COLD)
(18 years old)

Tonight Aidan and I fully committed to each other. We had a beautiful night in a snow cave he made just for us in the treeline that borders our houses. Sitting amongst the candles he had placed in the cave was like being surrounded by a thousand stars. We drank warm apple cider we had in a thermos. Then we decided to spend time at his folks' house because his mother was out of town.

I knew that a night like this one would be special and we had made a choice to wait until we were both 18 years old before making love. To say that I am not disappointed in the least would be an understatement. It was the single best night of my entire life and it was everything I had ever wanted it to be. I have never felt so connected to anyone. At times, I couldn't tell where my breath began and his ended.

Aiden is "the one" for me and always will be. I suppose saying he is my one and only true love sounds really lame and a bit cliché, but he is. I can't help it. I am ridiculously guilty of believing love is magical and the happily-ever-after is possible. Being with him makes me feel like life is somehow more alive in every way. Everything feels brighter, more cheerful and possible with him.

Now I allow myself to feel optimistic and the "what if's" no longer plague me throughout the day or steal my sleep at night.

I have spent so long fighting my mother and the other women in our family about their negative views that inevitable heartbreak comes when you fall in love with someone. Grandma went as far as reading tea leaves to predict the outcome of Aidan's and my relationship. She insists it won't last, but has no other details to give me. She just keeps saying that, "You will ruin it." Doesn't sound too divine to me.

What does Grandma know anyway? Despite her close connection and steadfast belief in the divine, she has nothing more to tell me than what I could have read in the horoscope section of the Sunday morning newspaper.

For four years, I have been insisting that Aidan and I are different. Love does not have to hurt. Love can feel wonderful and never go away. We are proof. I no longer feel I am living my mother's story or anyone else's. This is mine and I won't let the negativity of anyone squash this for me.

Just because I don't agree with my family, doesn't mean that I think Aidan and I are perfect. We always seem to work it out. That is the best part about him. He doesn't want any ugliness between us, even if it means one of us needs to swallow some pride and apologize for something we did first. We never apologize unless we mean it.

We have seen too many family members and friends get in relationships that seem to destroy them. It is heartbreaking and we have vowed to not act in the painful, horrible ways others have.

I don't see the two of us ever stopping our dance. I love Aidan with all my heart. Forever and always.

After reading this last passage, I decide I want to stop. Dan agrees with me. We hug for a long time. My appreciation for what we have is stronger than it was when he came back home with his things. I don't think we are as romantic or sappy as Grandma and Aidan, but I know we love one another. We just have to get out of our own way. Especially me. I think I take after the other women in the family more than Grandma. I still wonder why Dan wants to be with me and why I want to be with him. Could it be that we really were meant to be? Is this our dance?

Taking a breath, I feel the baby inside me kicking and I rub my belly. Gently, I take Dan's hand and place it there as well.

I want to take in this time with Sophie and Aidan and their story. I don't feel ready to jump to when things obviously went differently for them.

"Dan, I would like to check in with Grandma and Aidan downstairs and see what they are up to," I say.

Dan helps me up and we return to the library. We hear nothing. It is very quiet and I can't help feeling my face flush at the thought that maybe the two old love birds will be kissing away in their favorite room. Luckily, I am wrong. My feelings of possible embarrassment have now turned to concern.

Dan and I walk through the rooms and can't seem to find them anywhere. We begin to call out their names.

"Hey, Jori. I think I just found them. Look out there toward the pines."

As Dan points out the window toward the orchard, I see them walking hand in hand along the tree line bordering Aidan's childhood home. Of course, they would be outside. I feel a little silly missing an obvious explanation for their not being in the house.

Gazing out the window at old friends and untouchable love, I feel the last entry swirling around my head and heart. It was personal and intimate. Something I can actually see right now among the mountains, among the pines and apples. Something I will never forget.

3 p.m.

Sophie

*W*alking with Aidan outside is so wonderful. I am sure it won't be the last time we do this today. I love feeling his hand in mine and I can't help think about the regret of letting it go so easily. I am fifteen, sixteen, seventeen all over again. I feel like my feet are barely touching the ground.

As I breathe in, a thought of the past intrusively flashes through my mind. I see myself crying, angry. My chest feels like someone has been pounding on it all day. I hurt all over. I hate this thought. I don't want to think about pain or why I have a reason to have this thought. I squeeze Aidan's hand to help bring me back to the present, back to this moment in the sun, walking in the orchard toward our tree.

He immediately squeezes my hand back and I find that my breathing has been restored to a more natural and comfortable rhythm.

Aidan's arrival early this morning was overwhelming and amazing. There is still so much to tell one another and I can't wait to hear what else he has done over the years. I am not sure what to share with him about the direction my life went after we broke up. I am ashamed to admit that I didn't find the love I thought I would. I guess there is a part of me that still judges the choices I made about Ollie's father.

I am reminded of Ollie's father every day when I can't stay focused or have sudden gaps in my memory. As much as I try to laugh off the lapses when I'm around Jori or minimize them to try and protect myself from my own fear that I might permanently lose a memory, I know the truth. These blank spots are the consequence for staying as long as I did. If I hadn't had daily contact with my sister, Maggie Grace, I don't know what I would have done. She knew me better than anyone.

To talk about what Aiden and I felt with one another in the past and how we are feeling now, has led to the re-opening of old wounds and regrets. I am not just revisiting my time with Aidan, but the years I spent with Ollie's father as well.

"Hey, what's going on, Sophie?" Aidan asks me as he squeezes my hand again gently.

"Oh, you know me, Aidan, always thinking and working not to," I answer with a sad smile.

"Ah, I see. I do that, too. But I don't think we should care about what comes up anymore at our age. Maybe just for today, we can just trust that any thoughts are just fine."

"I think that's one of the best ideas I have heard in a long time. But I am not so sure that what comes up is what you want to hear, Aidan. Obviously a lot of time has gone by. We aren't the same. The truth is, we don't really know one another at all. Just what we remember and what we have imagined."

"Are you serious? Of course we know one another, Sophie. How else could we hold hands like this and walk together just as we used to. If we didn't, how would we even have this conversation? Listen, I think we are both aware that we have made choices and lived our lives the best we knew how. We still are doing so. Neither of us is perfect and never was. Please trust that what we share is okay and that there is no judgment from me, Sophie. I don't care what you tell me. I am not going to leave you ever again. I want you by my side regardless of where we are. Period."

"I know you are right, Aidan. Talking and being ourselves was never an issue between us. It's just that I never experienced that with anyone else but you. It has been so long since I've felt I can just be me with a man…I don't know what to do."

My sentence trails off and I begin sobbing. I try to finish my thought, "I don't know how to … Oh, I don't remember. I don't remember to trust being me without the fear of being hurt. I am so sorry, Aidan, that I am so damaged."

"Stop it, Sophie. Please don't say that about yourself." Aidan's beautiful eyes fill with tears and he strokes my arm. "I don't know what happened to you, Sophie, but I do know that you are still *you* in the most deepest parts of your spirit. No one can take that from you unless you let them. I am here. I will listen and I will still love you."

I allow Aidan to hug me, drifting off into the sense of comfort I have always had when he holds me. I make myself take some long, deep breaths and find the tears slow and stop. *I am okay. I am safe and I am loved.* I say this over and over to myself. My breathing becomes regular again. My consciousness tells me I am no longer holding my breath. My body softens into a relaxed state and I ask if Aidan will sit down on the blanket we brought with us. Gratefully, he agrees.

We steady each other as we lower our worn bodies to the ground. I am not concerned about getting back up. I simply don't care if this becomes my final resting place. Nowhere else has ever filled my spirit like this spot, and I have never liked spending time with anyone here as much as I do with Aidan.

Aidan leans up against the tree and I lay my head on his lap. I look around and up at the sky and allow the sun to warm the parts of me that feel sad and cold.

As I let the heartache I have been feeling drift away, I realize that regardless of my challenges, gratitude comes to my mind. Old hurts float away and I am brought to a present awareness of how blessed I am.

* * * * *

I can feel his heart filled with love as Aiden rests his eyes on me. I start to relax and breathe even more deeply. I begin to think about my walks in the orchard, day or night.

On my walks, I carry the same bag I have always take with me when I venture out. I have my candles, blanket, and a journal or two. Sometimes, I pull out one of Great-Grandma O'Neill's journals where she describes her journey from Ireland. Before each outing, I also bring my own journal, just in case I want to add a thought or two under the stars.

Gratitude fills me. Jori knows I need this sort of space to daydream or spend time just letting my mind wander to whichever memory calls to me most. She accommodates my needs so well and has grown accustomed to some of my more silly demands, like making sure I can walk through the orchard at night or along the tree line by the forest near my house as I always have. Her loving and concerned eye ensures me I make it in for the night.

Even though I am always a bit hesitant about removing anything from the trunk, since it protects and holds all the O'Neill women's journals, spanning at least four generations, I feel the power of the women through their writing. The trunk itself is special, but the contents and the stories it carries, both written and not, are what create this hesitation. The trunk has become iconic in our family. It is a physical reminder of our family's legacy before my ancestors came to Greenhill), and it was has seen us through decades of life's ups and downs.

I have so often envisioned images of my great-grandmother, Gratia, as she prepared to leave her home in Ireland, filling her trunk with her most prized possessions, praying that her determination and intuition would prove to be the compass she needed. She knew that whatever courage she had up to that point paled in comparison to what she had set in motion. Her courage would only have to grow beyond her current comprehension. Her faith would have to keep her on her path, regardless of the challenges she might face.

Her possessions were not simply things that held sentimental value, but rather items that could potentially keep her from harm as she traveled alone from County Clare, Ireland. Among those possessions were her special apple seeds, the legacy of the orchard from her homeland. She had no idea what lay ahead for her, but it was worth the risk, long planning, and an ocean voyage that lasted months before she reached New York City.

Once she arrived, a bit worn and miraculously alive amidst the dead and dying she saw on the ship, she quickly took the next steps of her journey, heading northeast. She encountered many people and experienced numerous towns throughout New England before she found her final place of rest in Greenhill, Vermont, which is where our family's roots were planted, where our legacy grew, and where it remains today.

Thinking of her sacrifices and the tremendous risks she took, I am deeply grateful. Even my saddest and most terrifying moments seem minor compared to what she faced. Knowing this has given me, given us, an unshakeable resolve to overcome whatever life has tossed our way. It has strengthened us beyond comprehension. Her legacy was her strength. I don't think this was her intent. It was simply what she did to have the kind of life that she could call good.

When we were children, Great-Grandmother Gratia's trunk provided many of us a hiding place and a special spot to keep some of our own most prized possessions, just as it had for her. It has had several different coats of paint to accommodate the creative urges so deeply ingrained in the women of our family, but only needed a few minor repairs, despite the many times it has been moved around. Surprisingly, it's still possible to see the original delicate floral paper that lines the inside walls.

As always, I digress. I believe I had started thinking about how much I enjoy my walks in the orchard and how wonderful Jori is.

What I love most, though, is sharing stories with Jori. I love to hear about her life as a student here in the local college, the challenges she has teaching her 2nd grade class, her love for Dan, her childhood sweetheart, and her excitement about their baby's arrival. She certainly has a lot on her plate.

I can't help but wonder if Aidan and I had figured out what Jori and Dan have already seemed to, would I have struggled so much with love in my life?

From time to time, Jori asks me questions about love and relationships, and I try not to give her too much advice. This is for a few reasons. First, I believe I made far more mistakes than I care to admit and don't feel exactly qualified to be the one to help her with one of the biggest decisions she will ever make about love.

Secondly, I don't want to meddle, but it is hard. I know she will have to learn the many lessons that love can bring. I suppose, to resist imposing my own opinions about what she should do, knowing she has to find her own way, I started relating stories from my life and those of the women in our family who have come before us, so Jori could draw her own conclusions about what to do.

As much as I love Jori, it wasn't always easy for us to talk to each other as she grew older. Our relationship changed and she was no longer enamored with me. Like her father, she began to see me as a person who had struggles and weaknesses just like anyone else. It is a right of passage for any teenager, but it was a challenging time for me. I wanted our relationship to be what it always had been. I watched over her, loved her, and she loved me without question, right back.

There was a time she moved away to go to college, closer to where her parents had relocated in the Midwest. I was conflicted about it. Happy for her, but resentful of being left alone again. Being resentful was not the way most people would characterize me, nor would I normally describe myself that way.

I have always prided myself on being a free spirit, independent and resourceful. If anything, I spent too much of my time being there for others and not for myself. I believe that's the reason I felt hurt; my life's purpose had become being there for my lovely granddaughter.

When Jori left Greenhill, I realized how much she had filled up my life. I wasn't sure what I would do without her. It had been a similar process with Ollie. One would have thought I would have become more insightful about the whole empty nest syndrome, but I didn't. I didn't think I would feel the same about my granddaughter as I had with my only son. But there I was, crying and stewing for days out of sheer self-pity. Which of course became irritability and detachment. I kept myself from wanting to communicate with her.

It took some time, but I finally managed to grow up a bit and get reacquainted with myself again. My oldest and dearest friend, Kat, would come for a visit for a week or two and we would act like kids all over again. Staying up at all hours of the night, laughing, still talking about the highs and lows of our lives, swimming, taking walks in the orchard, of course, and reminiscing.

Kat helped me gain some perspective when I felt I had lost it. She always had a way of telling me the truth without making me feel worse. It was such a gift. So when Jori first came back to Greenhill about four years ago, it was because my son suggested she needed to live here at the house full time. My resentment came back again despite my efforts to keep it at bay.

For the past four years, I had people coming and going here because I had rented out a room or two to college students who needed a place to stay. Sometimes it was because the college had miscalculated and assigned rooms they didn't have to returning students, or someone's financial aid hadn't quite covered all their expenses. My house was much cheaper than a room at a college dormitory.

During those short weeks before Jori returned, I relished the peace and quiet. I was annoyed with Ollie for making a plan like this without talking to me more. I think he assumed that because Jori and I had lived together most of her life, her transition would be seamless.

For another family perhaps, but not ours. We were far too stubborn at times—and irrational once we had been hurt. Jori's moving back was a process that needed careful planning and one that needed a wide wake of understanding as the two of us navigated the inevitable bumps.

Admittedly, I made her first few days with me unbearable. I was quick to snap at Jori and make comments I knew were hurtful. When I didn't directly interact with her, I simply ignored her, pretending she didn't even exist. I did what I wanted and when I wanted. I gave no regard to her needs.

For a while, I pretended I couldn't hear her just so she might grow frustrated from having to repeat herself several times. Hearing her call out my name louder and louder wouldn't make me budge. I even took things she had put away and placed them around the house, just to frustrate her and make her feel confused. Why not? I sure was! My behavior was outrageously childish, to say the least.

For some reason, her departure years before had hurt me in a way I hadn't felt in a long time. I went to a dark place. A place I hadn't been to in ages. The day she told me she was leaving, all I could hear was Ollie's father saying: "Why the hell would I stay with you? You have done nothing but be a pain in my ass! You are replaceable, you know."

It shook me deeply. I began getting weepy thinking of her leaving because of something I had done. I couldn't live with the fact that some action or statement of mine might have made her want to leave me. My mind turned and turned until I became a frenzied mess. I couldn't admit how insecure and pathetic I was for wanting her to stay and how much I loved her in my life.

It wasn't the same when Ollie left. Perhaps it is because he promised to return, which he did many times. Jori never indicated that I would see her again. At least not in a way I believed. Completely irrational, but it was how my brain thought at the time and how my heart felt.

When Ollie began renovations on the house and I learned that Jori was planning on coming back with Dan to start their married life together here on The Hill, I drove myself nuts on a different level with questions like: *Why did Ollie think Jori would want to live here anyway? What the hell did an old woman have to offer her?*

Ollie knew better and he certainly knew me better than I had thought. It was an old house that needed repairs, and I guess I needed some TLC as well. After renting it out for so long to the local college students, it had seen its share of better times. Those reasons did not stop Ollie from hiring a "small city" to restore and reconstruct the house on The Hill.

From the moment Ollie began his collegiate path in architecture, he had always talked about restoring the house entirely; not just a section here and there, which would have taken many years. It had become a mission. Saving our family home on The Hill motivated him in a way I had never seen.

Once he drew up the plans and reviewed them with me, it still took a lot more time for him to complete once he actually got started. I personally felt the project would never end. But I am selfish like that sometimes—only thinking about my needs and the impact a situation has on me (at least, that was what Ollie's father often told me). I suppose now with his daughter expecting her first child and her recent challenges with Dan, he figured he had better wrap up his plan sooner than later. Truth be told, I was happier than I have been for a very long time.

I realize my behavior was petty and ridiculous in so many ways. I thought at first I was angry, but then realized I had felt forgotten, so I didn't see why my house should be used by anyone but me. Isn't it me who had to take care of the hooligans my son called renters so they didn't completely tear down the house with their endless all-night comings and goings?

Ollie felt outraged every time renters wanted to break their leases early, knowing it was me who had pushed them to it. Having my temperament, he grew frustrated and referred to me as the "Queen of The Hill." It was a title I despised, since I used to do the same thing to my mother when I was angry with her. One thing can be said for traditions—they are consistent.

But other things concerned me. Jori had been gone a long time. The once familiar way we connected might never return. What if she didn't want it to? What if I couldn't stop hurting to let her back in?

Gratefully, Jori had a great deal of patience and it wasn't long before she caught on to what I was doing. She realized that I felt I was losing something dear to me and that not much attention had been paid to the home here on The Hill until Ollie decided Jori should live there again. She patiently waited for me to warm up to the change her presence had made in my home. Truth be told, it was just as much her home as it had been mine, my mother's, my grandmother's, and so on. Each of the O'Neill women had lived here. I can still see the stone wall that my Great-Grandmother Gratia built with her husband and brothers to create a boundary for our land.

As one might suspect, before long, I found great delight in talking with Jori. I felt less lonely with her around. She asked so many questions and seemed to have a real thirst for life and what it could teach you.

In some ways, Jori reminds me of myself. Strong-willed and yet so eager to learn. Having her stay here with me full time so that she could come and go more easily to attend her master's-level classes and still teach at the local elementary school was practically ingenious of Ollie. He knew the house would be an anchor for his daughter and her baby, as it has been for all of us. Jori needed to carry on our legacy in the Apple Tree Warrior spirit.

Jori and I have become quite close since her recent separation from her longtime love, Dan. It is hard to believe, but they have been two peas in a pod since they met in grade school. We all thought they had a special connection and never questioned that they would end up married and having children of their own. But as has happened with so many of the women in our family, the men simply don't always continue the journey with us.

My sister Maggie Grace was fond of saying, "They either die, leave, or find someone else who isn't so hard on them." A bitter sentiment that was more reflection of my sister's experience than all of ours, but there was a thread of truth in that love was not easy for us. We had great expectations, we were driven, and held strong views about life and how it ought to be lived. So, it seemed that we found partners who viewed these character traits as ones to be feared or controlled. Often we felt heartbroken or were afraid of the men we chose to be with. Unfortunately for me, it was both.

Well, maybe Jori will experience love differently. She is the one who pushed Dan away and asked him for the separation. Now that Jori is the last woman in our family tree, I think all of us are hoping she will rise above what too many of us could never completely do—be happy with ourselves and the ones we loved.

I admit we are hard women to get to know and it is no faint-hearted man or friend who has stayed with us. As timeless as the love Aidan and I share, I think the longest and happiest marriage goes to Great-Grandmother Gratia.

Once she arrived from Ireland to start her new life in New York and began traveling around New England to find what ultimately would become her home here in Greenhill, she met a young carpenter in Boston with whom she became friends. Not common for a woman to do in that era, but none of the women in our family have ever followed conventions very well. She decided before leaving Ireland that she would travel wherever she had to go and learn everything she would ever have to learn to be a self-reliant person. She never wanted to be completely dependent on a man, as had been the case with her mother and aunts.

Gratia always told us that she would have happily left this earth never having married if she had created the life she felt was true for her, instead of fabricating a life of lies so that others would approve of her. I always admired that and kept that sentiment close to my heart every time I felt weak or scared. To this day, I am amazed she did so well traveling unaccompanied for so long. Certainly, her Irish saints and guardian angels watched over her.

Great-Grandma left a legacy with her strength and perseverance to live life fully without regrets. She was at times the toughest one to spend time with. Her ability to speak and live the truth was difficult for others to take. Most folks hid behind their masks, but Gratia exposed their truth. She loathed gossip, although conflicts with others arose; they secretly admired her ability to do what they so often struggled to do for themselves.

Gratia's husband knew about her stubborn side and fierce independence before he courted her for more than three years. He knew that the woman he would spend the rest of his life with was not only the woman he always wanted to have by his side, but one who complimented his ideas about how he wanted to live his life. They called it "living the good life" and together, they created the foundation for our family. Together, they created the heart and soul of Greenhill.

Their wisdom and vision of having a community of innovative, hardworking, and creative people who would bring only prosperity to the town and to themselves is how Greenhill quickly became a visitor's home.

Gratia and her husband never held town or county positions. They never wanted any part of a political party or to participate in anyone's desire to use them to leverage themselves in such a manner. They kept life simple. They lived by example. I still don't entirely know how they managed it, but they did.

This new journey with Jori has been a wonderful addition in my life and today was no exception to the amazing ways it can feel like magic. Today she met us. An encounter I never expected her to have. She didn't know for sure what that would be like, when I found her crying early this morning, trying to find the answers to her current heartache, in one of our journals. Let's just say something was different that day, because I had felt tingly all over since last night, when I was picking apples from the orchard.

Jori only knew who Aidan was from the brief stories I had shared with her and from her brief interactions with him over the last few months. I don't think she truly knew the depth with which he had become one of the greatest experiences I had ever had with love.

Aidan came into my life in the strangest of ways. Both of us had suffered significant childhood losses and as our mothers worked to rebuild their lives, Aiden and I found solace in the orchard between our two houses. I had no idea how much our first encounter would begin to shape the long and, at times, confusing connection we had. How much he would touch such a deep part of my spirit.

I tried every logical explanation to justify our connection and even after all this time, it is like no other I have ever experienced. I suppose that is what makes our story so special to me and why I believe feeling great love changes your life.

Despite having lost time thinking of my grandmother and acknowledging my gratitude for my time spent with Jori, I gradually become aware of Aidan still gently stroking my hair and from time to time, using his fingers to softly trace the outline of my cheek along my jaw line.

I allow myself to fall back asleep, content and warmed by his touch and the sun that shines on us.

3 p.m.
Aidan

*S*itting here as Sophie sleeps is wonderful. I agree that we are not the same as we were when we last saw one another for obvious reasons, but walking hand in hand tells me that for the most part we still are. Having her rest her head on my lap and feel her body let go as she enters a deeper, more restful sleep is exactly as I imagined we would spend part of our day.

I can see how troubled she became today and I can't assure her enough that I am more than ready to hear whatever she wants to share with me.

Some months ago, I spent some time with Maggie Grace. Sophie and Jori are not aware of this. I was fortunate to have connected with Jori, but Maggie Grace was really the key to my determining if seeing Sophie was a good idea. She knew Sophie better than anyone and I felt that talking with Maggie Grace was the only way to be absolutely sure I would not cause more harm than good.

We met a few towns over on her farm about two months before I planned to return to Greenhill permanently. Similar to Sophie, it felt easy to see Maggie Grace again and yet, I felt nervous. The O'Neill women are intense and full of life. They can be loving and warm, but can be cold and distant when they feel wronged by someone. It is this energy that has always drawn me to Sophie and her family. It is a fairly simple life philosophy that is not much different than my own.

Any coldness or distance they felt toward someone was not impulsive nor vengeful. It would take a lot to get them to not want a person in their life. You know that if that is where you landed, you must have made some serious transgressions.

Maggie Grace was hesitant throughout our conversation, trying to be careful about sharing too much. She explained that it was her sister, Sophie, who needed to decide how and when she shared what she wanted about her life after she and I had parted ways. I respected that and didn't pry.

I learned that Sophie had married and it was that relationship that almost broke the woman I have resting on my lap.

"It wasn't good, Aidan. That is all I will say right now," is what Maggie Grace said. "She suffered far more than we realized until it was almost too late. Although she came back to us, it was clear she was not the same Sophie. An old injury resurfaced and her memory was not what it used to be. It is irreversible, unpredictable, and at times almost impossible to understand. She explained that Sophie had all her short- and long-term memory, but it is not accessible the way it is for the rest of us. Under stress, her short-term memory is almost non-existent. And the long-term memory can often get mixed with the present day.

Maggie Grace continued. "Sometimes she has several minutes, as if she were experiencing something from two, five, or even thirty years ago. You can't tell her it isn't happening, only to go along with it. Once the recollection passes, she has a vague idea that something happened, but Sophie usually just thinks she got lost in a thought. She doesn't know she is reliving a moment. Again, we don't tell her which, just try to help her. Most often, the worst episodes are around Ollie's father."

Hearing about Sophie's memory challenges, I had another reason to be concerned about approaching her. The doctors explained that with a brain injury like Sophie's, coupled with the post-traumatic stress she had due to her experiences with Ollie's father, it would be a lifelong challenge for her. I didn't want to trigger a negative reaction if she were to see me.

Again, Jori was great about helping. Over the past few months, she carefully found a way to bring up my name, trying to gauge how Sophie consistently reacted. Jori observed any obvious reactions in the moments she mentioned me and even days after. After doing this for quite some time and seeing nothing adverse occur, we agreed that it was probably okay for me to return to Sophie's life.

This morning and this day, we were proven right.

I meant what I said to Sophie about not judging her for whatever she may have done or experienced since our break-up, but I will admit I am scared to hear about what happened to her. Will I be able to comfort her enough? Will she know just how much I care for her, even though clearly the things she tells me might shock or upset me?

I feel Sophie begin to stir as she shifts her head and mumbles something.

"Sophie? Are you awake?"

Groggily, she smiles and says, "I think I am, Aidan."

I gently help her sit up and her long, thick hair falls in disheveled waves around her face and down the left side of her body. She is so beautiful.

"Did you fall asleep, too, Aidan?" she asks softly.

"Sort of. I drifted in and out. I just didn't want to stop looking around at the mountains and you. I didn't want to miss one moment of this beautiful day."

"You are so corny, Aidan," Sophie playfully laughs.

Hearing her laugh makes me laugh too, and the next thing I know, I am tearing up. It is the same laugh that made me so curious about her and I am overwhelmed with how great it is to hear it again and to know that she didn't lose it.

"I think we better go check on Jori and Dan. I am sure they are wondering what we oldsters have been doing out here for so long. They probably think we kicked the bucket or something."

Laughing again, Sophie and I help one another up and begin walking slowly back to the house, hand in hand.

"Hey, you two!" Jori shouts from the back porch. "About time you two came back in. Dan and I made a late afternoon lunch."

"Good Lord, Jori, you'd better give birth soon. None of us are going to be able to see past our toes the way you keep making so much great food," Sophie calls back.

"Amen to that, Sophie!" Dan shouts back as he pats his stomach.

"Wait! It is great, isn't it?" Sophie adds.

By then, Sophie and I have made it back to the porch and find the perfect spot on the wicker sofa. Spread before us is an array of cold cuts, fresh fruit, cheese and crackers, and some fresh, ice-cold apple cider.

After filling our plates and pouring glasses of cider, I enjoy the chatter that has begun between Dan and Jori about what they want to make sure they get done before their baby arrives in the next couple of weeks.

Eventually, the talking quiets to a natural and peaceful pause and I feel Sophie squeeze my hand. I look over and give her a kiss on her cheek.

Jori speaks up and says, "Okay, I can't understand it. I don't get how after all these years and your age, I am sitting here feeling like I should excuse myself to leave you two alone. There is no doubt you love each other and every time I look over at the two of you, I feel like I am the third wheel."

"You are!" Sophie and I say in unison. We each let out a small laugh.

"Don't worry, Jori. This is the way it always was with us. A lot of folks said that to us when we were together. I think Sophie and I just have our own special place we go to together. I don't think we are or were ever quite conscious of when that happened or how much except when others pointed it out."

"I am glad I am not the only one then," Jori says.

"Certainly not," Sophie replies.

"Grandma, Aidan?" Jori asks. "Do you think you can tell us now what happened between the two of you?"

Aiden replied, "Sure. It is simple really. We were young, driven, and didn't understand how to fit the other into the goals we individually made for our life." I reply with a wave of my hand. "Nor did we have the life experience to truly understand how to compromise. Add in stubbornness and making assumptions and you have the two us walking in completely different directions."

"Well said, Aidan. I don't think I could have put it that eloquently." Sophie nods in assent.

"Good, I am glad you think so, Sophie. I hope you know that I was only speaking from my perspective," I murmur, patting her lovely hand reassuringly.

"I know. Thank you, Aidan." Sophie looks over at Jori and Dan, and sees that our words have still not satisfied their curiosity.

"Jori, upstairs you and Dan go. I know you already organized my journals, so get to the next one. When you finish with that one, you should see a series of journals. They are all the same gray color and size. Don't come down until you read each one. Then, when you want to talk, you will find me down here with Aidan. Most likely sleeping again, but please wake me up."

"Okay, Grandma. See you soon." Jori and Dan get up and head inside.

Sophie sighs. I know this is part of the next step she needs to guide Jori toward. But I don't think it is as much about telling her our story, or even what occurred between Sophie and Ollie's father, as it is about letting go.

4 p.m.

Sophie

I sigh as I watch Jori and Dan make their way into the house to where they will discover how it felt for me when Aidan and I parted ways. It is also where they will learn about me and Ollie's father. I already talked to Ollie this morning regarding Jori's curiosity regarding events between the grandfather she never met and the only father my son ever knew.

Ollie agreed to let her read the gray journals and had reached out to her to let her know that if she wanted to talk to him about their contents, she could. I let him read those journals long ago, when he had questions and needed some closure, as well as guidance about the kind of man he was becoming and ultimately wanted to be.

I squeeze Aidan's hand and feel it is time for me to tell him about what life was like for me after we broke up and the subsequent journey I took.

"Aidan, I want you to know that what I share is about what I felt after we parted ways. The choices I made were just that. Mine. Are you sure you are okay with what I want to share?"

"Of course, Sophie. I love you and that means knowing all parts of you. I thought I had always shown you that."

"You did and are, Aidan. I think that when you hear more, you will understand it is not about what you have done, Aidan. It is about what I did, the life I led for years, and the impact that had on me. I also want to make sure you know that I will work to remember as much as I can. I am not sure if Maggie Grace told you or not, but sometimes, I simply can't keep a consistent thought going. I suddenly blank out or the things I am thinking about are not always tied to the present. It is not intentional and to be honest, I am not entirely sure why it happens, but it has for years, I guess. At least it feels that way. Who knows, it has probably has only been going on for a few weeks. I suppose it is just part of getting old for me."

"I have no concerns, Sophie. Tell me what you need to and I will listen," Aiden says.

Sighing again, I feel myself letting go of the present, drift into the past, and allow that old heartache of our break-up replay in my mind...

* * * * *

*A*idan and I had many nights together, getting to know each other intimately on so many levels as we emerged from early childhood friends, high-school sweethearts, and now college lovers. He asked deep and soulful questions about who I thought I was and where I felt I was going. He always wanted to know the parts of me that couldn't be seen.

I searched for what lay behind his deep, hazel-brown eyes and their many expressions. We continued to share some of the highlights of our greatest life experiences we had had so far in our young lives and some of the wounds that had been tucked away from times past, like the fact that both of our fathers had abandoned their families. We shared everything, from memories about our childhoods to our very first crushes.

We talked about God and religion. We talked about values and bonds we had with our family and friends. Moments we felt betrayed and how we had learned how to forgive. More than ever, I was convinced that Aidan and I were meant to be together. Any doubts I had were completely gone. I simply sank into this blissful state and I had no idea just how deep I had gotten myself into this relationship and how much I was learning about love. How much I was learning about life. It was wonderful.

School and work kept me so very busy. I still had to keep juggling my full-time course load and a full-time job. I had taken on some additional responsibilities at school with a few leadership positions on campus, which took up more time than I probably should have let them, but I was determined to get a great job out in world, even though I couldn't imagine saying goodbye to a community that had always been a home to me and a family in every fiber of my being.

I wasn't the only one who felt this way. Greenhill always seemed to have that effect on people. Even on people who didn't grow up here. Locals who swore they would never return were the ones who moved back the fastest once they were married and decided to start a family. Ironic, really. I can't help but think how our parents, who did the same thing, must just shake their heads every time someone says, "I am so out of here and never coming back!"

As May graduation approached, you could feel the campus and the town changing. With the last few weeks rapidly flying by, most of the conversations around campus were about how no one felt really ready to leave and trying to decide what types of jobs graduates would have once they left college. The world was our oyster, yet none of us was quite sure we wanted to jump into the sea.

I was beginning to feel that pull toward a new life, imagining the places I would travel, while the old life blocked me from fully embracing the potential I had. Looking at my family and our home, and now with my relationship with Aidan, I was reminded of what I would have to leave behind. I wanted comfort in the midst of all that was coming.

It was hard for me to explain to Aidan why I was concerned. It was easier to think it was just the weariness of my personality to which I often gravitated when changes were in the air. I also felt that our relationship had been moving along so fast that we hadn't really thought about what the future might hold for us. For our connection, a connection neither of us knew how to describe.

Yes, something bigger than I knew had nestled its way into my spirit and I barely noticed it. I believe it started with Aidan talking about the kind of life he wanted to live. I was intrigued by the idea that there was much more to life than surviving. Life as a celebration? Life by design? When did I become so serious?

Most of my time had been spent just trying to get through each day, often trying to prepare myself for what might be coming next, often not expecting the best. I secretly wished somehow life would surprise me, without my having to do a whole lot—at least once.

Ironically, Aidan had become unbelievably adept at being in the moment. I was completely clueless on how to do this. In fact, he was so good that when I brought up my concerns about life after our graduation and where that would take us, he didn't have much to say except, "Let's just enjoy the time we have here together, Sophie. Why worry about tomorrow? Aren't things going great between us?"

I didn't know how to answer questions like that. I didn't know what he meant by not worrying, because anxiety had crept in and had become so second nature to me. Were my grandmother's tea leaf prophecies actually possible? Should I just enjoy the time we have now because it wouldn't last? Bothering to worry about the future seemed silly in hindsight, but that's what I did most days and nights.

Often, during our conversations about our future together, a knot would form in my stomach, sending waves of nausea throughout my body. I knew so much was changing within me and I didn't have control over it at all. Feeling like a small ship drifting into the roaring sea, my grip on everything I had come to know started moving me in an unknown current. Dealing with the growing connection between Aidan and me excited and thrilled me beyond words, yet scared me, too. What was I going to do? I didn't want to lose what Aiden and I had, as my mother had lost my father so many years ago.

4 p.m.

Jori

Dan and I return to Sophie's journals and are able to easily find the one she said we needed to read next. I am excited, but also feel sadness seep in. I know the obvious: she and Aidan do break up. But I also know that reading the intimate details in her journal bring that truth to a different level of intimacy, one that most never really hear or see.

Carefully, I open up the worn, tan, leather-bound book and in silence, Dan and I both begin reading...

Sophie's Journal
(College—almost 20!)

I can barely stand myself these days. All I do is count the numbers of days left before Aiden leaves. I asked him why he decided he had to go to Washington anyway.

His reply: "Sophie, you know better than anyone why I feel I need to go. It is only for six months and then I will be back and we can start planning where we want to live when we graduate. Besides, you will have a new job, school and The Hill to manage. That will keep you so busy, you probably won't even think about me that much...ha ha. Right?"

"Yeah, right, Aidan...I won't think of you much at all," I said to him. I know I won't die or anything from Aidan's being gone. It's just that I really enjoy him and his company. I don't want to lose him like my mom lost my dad. Like my grandmother said I would lose him.

Aidan is right that being called to a place and to an experience is such a gift. He has to go. It is unfair for me to try and make Aidan choose between me and his new adventure. The fact that he wants me to join him is great, but I can't. Not now. I simply don't want to be separated from him that long. I want him to stick to our plan to leave Greenhill together.

Something feels strange about it. I can't explain. In my heart, I know this is important for him and I don't want to interfere with it. But how do I let my fear go? How do I take responsibility for my growing insecurities and questions about what is really between us? How can....

I am tired and weary from all my thinking and the roller coaster of emotions. I must have fallen asleep writing with a heavy heart. With the date of Aidan's departure clearly coming faster than I want, I have developed a daily ritual of trying to feel gratitude for each moment I have with him, conscious that these moments will be most fresh in our hearts and spirits when we miss one another once he leaves. Trying to keep my intentions light and cheerful, I have decided to draw him a picture of our tree to take with him. It is a great distraction and I have picked a challenging medium to work with—watercolor. Not one I often use.

Pausing for a moment, Jori and Dan look at each other and both start to ask a question.

Laughing, Dan says, "You go first, Jori."

"Okay, thanks, not sure what exactly to ask first. I guess I didn't expect to read what led up to the break-up. I was thinking we were going to go head first into the break-up and all that entailed."

"I've got to admit, I did, too." Dan says.

"So are you getting what I am? That Sophie and Aidan were making plans to stay together, but Sophie was more resistant to leaving than Aidan had anticipated?"

"Yes. That sounds about right," Dan confirms.

"Well, let's keep reading and see what else we find out." Jori slides her finger down the page to the place they left off.

Every day, despite feeling tired from work, I sketch and paint until my back and neck start to cramp with small spasms from being held awkwardly for so long. He doesn't know I am doing this and I can't wait to surprise him!

I feel this painting couldn't be more perfect and so I pour all my heart into it. Besides, I don't want him to have to remember all the times we bickered or when I became sulky and glum about his departure. I want him to feel my joy and support. I also let in his patient words to "hang in there" help me put away all my concerns, deep inside me. He as even asked me several times to come out to visit him at least once, after he gets settled in.

As much as I know I will miss him, I just can't see it. This is where "we" are and belong. I don't want to try and fit into his life; I want the one we have here together, now.

I have been trying to not let Aidan know just how truly unsure I am about what will happen between us once he leaves. In trying to convince him, and more importantly myself, I find that I dive deeper into denial. When we make love, I push away thoughts that this will be the last time I will have with him like this and I smile when I want to cry. I think it is working because I can see Aidan is not so tense when we spend time together.

Somehow, not only have I been able to fool him, but this small charade has even given me a break from my worries. In fact, I have gone as far as teasing myself when we are together appearing that I know how silly I am being for worrying about the future.

Alone late at night or on my walks through the orchard, I can't escape what I really feel. I spend a lot of time sobbing by myself. Ashamed of my insecurities and my desire to cling to Aidan, I chastise myself by pointing out that there are greater tragedies than a boyfriend leaving for a few months. It is not like what happened with Dad. It is not like I won't see him again for years.

But my grandmother's words and my mother's cautionary looks and comments make me feel like I am dodging an outcome I cannot change or control despite my efforts to do both. I am not ready to let go.

The reality is that Aidan and I are changing. The safety of Greenhill, our tree, and the years in which we connected to one another are no longer there for us. The reality is that our own changes mean that we can't stay the same. And the magic of the places we once shared will not be seen or felt in the same way ever again.

Now there is no place for us as we part physically, clear across the country. And now I am admitting for the first time, I don't ever recall the tea leaves being wrong. I don't understand that. Why had we met at the wrong time?

Dan and I look at one another. The next entry is more detailed and intense than what we have read so far...

It is 2 a.m. and I can't sleep and so I decide to write again. Aidan has now been gone for several weeks and we have a consistent schedule when we call one another. We struggled for a little while as Aidan got settled into his routine and coordinating the time difference between us.

Despite our weekly phone calls, it still doesn't feel like enough. But how could it? I know I am being stubborn, but I don't want to fly out to see him. Despite his pleadings and frustration that I complain but won't do anything about it, I can't explain to him that I don't know why I feel frozen in staying back here. Maybe I am just a big ole coward who likes to complain after all.

I have been busy trying to work on my class work and my job in town. I am still debating on my next step in terms of my major.

The longer Aiden is gone, the easier it is in some ways to have this new life. It feels bittersweet. The distance between us is becoming more evident and I realize clearly it is not just geographical. Time spent talking on the phone is usually about the classes he is taking or learning about the impact that developing communities are having on the natural environment and of course, the latest escapades he and his new friends have been on.

I spend a lot of energy trying to make my life here in Greenhill sound exciting, because it feels so boring compared to his experiences. I have been working hard on finding ways to keep myself occupied so as to not think of him so much. I have even had a couple of offers to go out on dates, but of course I don't want to be with anyone but Aidan and certainly don't want to cause more concern to Aidan by sharing this with him.

I don't know what to do with the disappointment I often feel once we hang up. I can't help sensing the gap growing between us and not knowing how to talk about it or if it is even important to do so. Maybe once he comes back I will forget about all this angst. I certainly hope so. Late at night, I can hear him whisper in my ear, "*You haven't left my mind, not even for a second.*"

Sophie's Journal
(6 months are done!)

I am so excited, I can't sleep! I can't wait to pick up Aidan tomorrow from the airport! I am so glad I have to work during the day so I won't spend every moment counting down the minutes until I see him.

His flight won't come in until almost 8 p.m. or so. Wow! I never thought this day would come. He wasn't supposed to return for another two weeks, but it appears things have changed! I can't wait to see him. I can already feel my insides fluttering with excitement as I see him walking toward me through the airline gate!

Best of all, we have planned the next week or so to be together before he begins a new field placement just a few towns over from Greenhill. I can't wait to smell him and feel his arms hugging me tight once again. We just talked earlier today, confirming his flight information and he can't wait to see me, either. All that worrying for nothing!

Everything feels like it is going to be great! Aidan was right; I need to trust more. Well, I will work on it, dear Aidan, I will work on it.

I sense a presence in the room and look up to see Sophie in the doorway. "Grandma! I am so glad you joined us."

"I thought I would check on you for just a moment. Just to see how far along you two were in the journals.

There are a lot. As you know, I have never been brief when it comes to talking about experiences that come so deeply from my heart."

"I am not much better," Aidan grins, standing beside Sophie.

Sophie gives Aidan a hug and continues to share her feelings about those unsettled times with Dan and me.

"After about a week of Aidan's being home, I started feeling tense again," Sophie begins. "I didn't know how to let things be. Aidan and I had shared so much together, but now his new experiences stood between us, and I couldn't relate as well. This caused a lot of tension and bickering.

"It wasn't long before Aidan finally shared that the reason he came back a couple weeks earlier than we had planned was because they had offered him an additional eight months in Washington, meaning he would be gone for more than a year. That would replace a lot of the academic credits needed to finish his degree and he would be creating the potential for a guaranteed spot in their architecture firm.

"I was stunned. So happy, sad, and angry at once that I couldn't speak at all when he told me. Aidan did everything anyone could have asked for; he was patient and of course, again asked me to join him.

"I took my time answering, but when I did, it was a firm 'no.' I wasn't leaving and now that he had changed his plans, I felt thoroughly betrayed. I was not willing to wait for him, as I was certain he would surprise me with yet another change of plans.

"Knowing that waiting for one another would be back at some point, we were growing apart to pursue our personal goals and dreams and despite what we said we wanted, our actions clearly did not align.

"Of course, there is no one really to blame. It was the choices we both had made that created that," Sophie concluded.

Quietly, Aidan begins to share with Dan and me as well.

"I wanted to believe we could pick up where we had left off. Sophie, I hadn't anticipated feeling like your life was now very separate from mine. It made what I was about to tell you that much harder and in some small way, that much easier, too.

"I had a started a new life in Washington to finish my coursework and field placement and Sophie was learning her new course work in Art Therapy. Our differences felt like a gigantic chasm, with little light to guide us. Boy, did we want to please one another. I think that intention kept us hopeful and excited about the possibilities of staying together at first. But the offer of an additional eight months in Washington only delayed our plans."

Sophie places her slender hand on Aiden's sleeve and continues. "Some days, I found that I all I could think about was my life with Aidan and on other days, I was a vibrant, smart, resourceful, young, educated woman who shouldn't be overly concerned with a serious relationship right now.

"Aiden and I went to dinner, maybe a party or two, and would fall asleep exhausted. No more in-depth, soul-searching conversations late at night or making love like we once used to. He kept telling me he didn't want to let me go, but I recognized that he was not going to allow me in any farther than we had already gone. I didn't let him in, either.

"He said he knew that his return was really to spend time with me and prepare for another goodbye. Perhaps even a permanent one. He had already spoken to his parents, who understood how much he wanted to take advantage of the opportunity in Washington, but talking to me would be much harder. He was so right.

Sophie gathers herself before going on. "That pulling away hurt and frightened me, and so with my cutting words and sometimes with a brief look, I became mean. I couldn't seem to resist and continued to use my breaking heart as an excuse. In the few short days Aidan had been home, the roller-coaster ride seemed only to have gotten more bumpy. He would be leaving again within a few days. I felt as if my doubts about the distance between us had been confirmed.

"Aiden's changing his mind and staying longer in Washington had altered something for me. Of course, it is natural to change your mind or plans, but why he hadn't thought about talking to me about it felt weird. Despite our connection, I had somehow missed this course alteration completely.

A slight sadness is now present in the room as Aidan, Sophie, Dan, and Jori sit in the nursery. Jori decided to get up and move around.

Eventually, Aidan breaks the silence with, "We always knew one another so differently than the other people we spent time with. It was so magical, Sophie. Can you really blame us for not wanting to let go?"

"Of course not," Sophie sighs.

"In our hearts, we knew the truth. Our intuition always guided us in this dance," Sophie says.

"Yes, it has, but we didn't always listen to it, did we?" Aidan replies in his soft voice.

"No, I suppose we didn't. I do have regrets about that, Aidan."

"As do I, Sophie."

Not knowing what else to say and to shift the heaviness in the room, I say quietly, "I think I better check on dinner. It is definitely time for me to eat." Dan takes her arm and guides her down the stairs.

Sophie remains seated in the old rocking chair, while Aiden has pulled up a footstool to be near her. They stay behind in the baby's room, a symbol of a new beginning. They glance at the open journal and start reading together.

Sophie's Journal
(Summer)

Well, I am here with Aidan at the beach enjoying the beautiful cloudless day. It almost looks like a painting, the sky is so blue and sunny today. It is unbelievably hot and I am about to go into the waves for a quick, refreshing dunk.

Looking over at Aidan sleeping under the willow tree here at the lake, I am sometimes in awe of what we have together. It feels like pure magic. We made it these last few months with his being gone again and celebrating his brief time off couldn't have been any more wonderful!

I look back at the moments that brought Aidan and me together. To feel this level of passion so young and not have limits as to what we share and talk about is almost indescribable. If he said he wanted to fly to the moon someday, I wouldn't think twice about it and I don't think he would find it strange that I want our first house to be in a tree!

Being around Aidan makes me want to dream even more and let go of fears about life. I love that we can share our dreams and passions with each other without feeling judged or questioned.

Now that Aidan has officially outlined the remaining time he has so that he can complete his degree, I am looking forward to our being together more and figuring out a way to make this work.

For my part I know nothing with any certainty,
but the sight of the stars makes me dream.
—Vincent VanGogh

5 p.m.

Aidan

*A*s I sit with Sophie, lightly holding her hand, I recall our last conversation as if it were yesterday.

Reflecting on that fateful moment so vividly, I remember our passionate exchange.

"Why do you have to be like this, Sophie?! Why can't you see that nothing, I mean absolutely nothing, has changed between us. I am still here.!"

"Bullshit! This is just part of your exit plan. You knew I wouldn't go with you. You knew that even if I did want to go, I wouldn't be able to . My life is here. It is with my family. I can't just leave The Hill! You KNOW THAT! I can't believe how selfish you are to ask me to go with you, knowing I can't!"

"No, Sophie, the fact is you won't AND that is your choice. I have to figure out what I want. I didn't plan on falling so in love with Washington that I don't want to leave. Isn't this what we said we would do? That we would find a home for us outside of Greenhill? To explore? I don't get what the problem is. This is a dream come true for me. No one gets accepted into a firm like this before I'm even done with college. I can't say no and I don't want to."

Sophie just stares at me with a cold rage I have never seen on her face before. I don't care. She is ridiculously rigid and uncompromising. God forbid anything changes. My anger starts to come to the surface, which, of course, is the worst time to talk to anyone, but I can't resist. I am angry, hurt, and I want her to understand me. So I forge on.

"I don't have a family legacy to fall back on if my dreams don't work out, like you do." Thick with sarcasm and drenched in hurt. Hurt that I want pointed directly at her.

Sophie becomes quiet and when she speaks, it is eerily calm and slow. "Get out and don't ever come back. I don't care what you do and who you do what with. You are selfish and you absolutely disgust me. How dare you hold my own family against me? You are not some loser, Aidan, who won't ever have another opportunity to do something great. I am not going to sit here waiting like some pathetic love-struck girl. Obviously you haven't gotten the message that I am nobody's doormat!"

"You have completely lost your mind, Sophie! I have never thought that way about you nor would I expect you to do nothing for your life and your dreams while I pursue mine. So what that the timing is a little off? So what that we didn't do this exactly like we talked about? The point is that our dreams are coming true and I want you there with me. Has nothing of the last five years meant anything to you? Is this it? It's over if I go?"

"Don't turn this around on me, Aidan! You went ahead and applied for this and never told me. We never had a chance to talk about the 'what if's'... Now that this is happening, you want me to suddenly do what you want and if I don't, then I am someone who has lost her mind? What happened to OUR dream of finding OUR home together? You went ahead and paved the way without me. Why should it matter now that I am with you? You have already been living in Washington for almost a year and I have waited and waited so that we could begin our plan and now apparently it is just your plan.

"I think you'd better take a good, hard look at that, Aidan. What happened to OUR plan? What happened to graduating together and picking out a place to start our life together? What happened to our plan to drive across the United States to see if we could find that one place that felt like home to us outside of Greenhill? You have changed everything! I am done. Get out and I don't care what happens to you and your stupid dreams."

I am shattered and feel completely broken. I can't believe what she just said to me and I can't believe that if I had spoken, I might have said something I would regret even more. My legs won't move and there is an odd sensation of numbness and heaviness that keeps me from doing so.

Closing my eyes, I will my legs to move. I gather my senses enough and turn away. After taking my first step away from Sophie, I say, "I will always love you, Sophie. Always."

I have no idea if she heard me and if she did, that she even cared. Only silence followed me through the remnants of the orchard and along the tree line to my house. It was the most deafening silence I had ever experienced.

Although I never told her to wait, I realize that was exactly what I had been asking her to do. I wasn't ready for us to find our home. It was clear that I needed to do my own dreaming for a while. I just didn't want to let go.

I had deceived her. I had deceived myself so I didn't have to let her go. I didn't want to break her heart like her dad had, and so I smiled when I wanted to cry and I hugged her as I wanted to walk away.

Sophie was right. I had betrayed her and I couldn't lie anymore. She had known the deeper truth. I wasn't ready for a life-long commitment to her or anyone except me.

Part Three

Evening

6 p.m.

Sophie

*L*istening to Aidan recount our break-up was painful. It was true I had said all those things and the shame of being mean remains today. It is that shame I carried with me as I dove into dating after Aidan and I parted ways. I wasn't looking for anything serious and that is exactly what I got. A bunch of first and second dates.

It was the same story every time. The guy would tell me I was a pretty girl, a sweet girl but ... well, fill in the blank. Wish I lived closer, had a more conventional plan for my future, didn't have so many family obligations. One man actually said he thought I should exercise more. I didn't take his words too seriously, given that I ran almost three miles every day and just because I didn't share his passion for becoming a triathlete, didn't mean I needed to work out more.

After a year of this kind of dating, I met Ollie's father. It was at a mid-week dinner gathering with some of my new friends from work. He was charming and handsome and incredibly easy to talk to. I don't think he ever met a stranger. He was interesting and funny and all I could think about that night is how much I wanted to keep talking with him. I got my wish. As I prepared to leave, he boldly came up to me and said, "I think I need to take you on a date."

"I think you do, too," is all I said and before I knew it, I was completely enamored with an amazing, smart, and handsome man. He wasn't overly romantic with extravagant gifts or outings. But he was a master with words. "I was perfect" is what he said. He wouldn't change a thing about me. I was his "soul mate," the only one who ever really knew who he was deep inside. I felt like I had hit the jackpot. I had finally met my "forever guy."

The gifts he brought me were thoughtful. A pen or paint I mentioned I'd like to try or use for my art work. You would have thought he had promised me a trip to Europe or that these small gifts were expensive jewelry. But they weren't and I didn't care. I had always appreciated the type of things that meant something, not just what the dollar sign attached to them might be. He wrote sweet notes about how much he loved the way I supported his dreams and ideas and how much he couldn't wait to marry me.

It was easy to be with him in the first few weeks of dating. I would wake up and find that I couldn't wait to talk to him, to discover what we might be able to do together that day despite our demanding work schedules. He was getting his master's degree in counseling with a specialty in addictions, and I had begun work at a local art studio. I was busy teaching classes to young adults and working on my own art pieces for the various shows and festivals around New England, where I was selling my art.

I wanted to have my own art studio within the next year or so and worked long days and sometimes nights trying to get ahead faster. Of course, I continued to keep the accounting books for The Hill. The orchard had grown and happily, my mother finally listened to me and my sister and expanded our small gift shop. It was a typical New England gift shop with all the expected novelties. Maple sugar candy, postcards, prints of the landscape sprinkled with cows, various flavors of cheese made on local farms, and of course, some of our family's bread and apple chutney. The charming shop was a hit with tourists and served as an outlet where some of the locals sold their products, too. But it was a lot of work!

Ollie's father loved everything I did, he said. He couldn't believe what an amazing and independent woman I was. He had already mentioned how his last relationship felt like he had had a boat anchor around his neck the whole time. He mentioned that Sarah, his ex, had been nothing but a leech and never seemed to stick with any particular job or interest. It felt good that he didn't have to worry about that with me. And I was happy to show how much I could do without ever burdening him.

The first few weeks together were fun and simply wonderful in every way you might imagine a new relationship would be. Aiden had finally left my thoughts and I slowly stopped feeling like I was walking in that new lovestruck haze. It felt really, really good to be so liked and feel attractive to a man again. In those early days, Ollie's father always seemed to know what to say and when to say it and his words would last for days in my heart.

About two months into dating, we went out with some of Ollie's father's friends for a drink at the local pub, a favorite of townspeople and visitors alike. It featured one of our local brewer's ale and was a laid-back place to listen to live music and relax. The food was good, too. I never could pass up a small crock of their shepherd's pie. When I found out we were going, I made sure I hadn't eaten much that day so that I wouldn't feel guilty eating the tender chunks of meat surrounded by thick gravy, potatoes, and vegetables smothered in butter and rich beef juices. "Heaven in a bowl" is what we called it.

Happily talking and laughing amongst friends, one of Ollie's father's buddies remarked that he was glad to see his old friend laughing again and even better was seeing him with a great gal like me in his life. Smiling, I looked at Ollie's father and thanked his friend for being so kind. Although Ollie's father was smiling and had squeezed my arm lovingly, I saw a flash of darkness in his eyes. Anger and sadness.

Wondering if I had imagined what I just saw, I quickly said to our group, "Well, I am glad to be here as well." I hoped my words would diffuse whatever I noticed shift in Ollie's father's eyes. And it did briefly.

As the evening progressed, Ollie's father became more aloof. He continued to drink like the rest of us, but it seemed that he finished each beer a little more quickly. Before I could think of ordering another drink, one was waiting for me. Suddenly, the room seemed to get incredibly loud and hot and I couldn't quite stop the room from slowly spinning.

I nudged Ollie's father and told him I needed to get some air. "I think I need to go home."

Coolly, he said, "Yes, I think you do."

He helped me off the stool and quickly, we said our goodbyes. The room felt slippery and full of sludge as I tried to maintain my footing and bearings. He didn't say a word to me once we found his car. We had planned on going back to his apartment that night so I was grateful I didn't have to deal with my mother's looks when I entered the house on The Hill. My mother never wanted to see her daughters intoxicated to the point that they needed help walking. She had seen her fair share of alcoholism in our family and hoped her daughters wouldn't go down that road.

I rolled down his car window and let the cool night air sober me up. Instantly, I began to feel better and the silence in the car helped me focus more, too. My senses were gradually returning to a somewhat normal range. I also saw that Ollie's father's mood had darkened again; this time, there was no question.

"Are you upset with me?" I asked softly and with some hesitation. No response. I waited and the next fifteen minutes in the car felt like hours. Then I thought, *Maybe he hadn't heard me. Don't read into his feelings, Sophie*, I told myself. But my anxiety got the best of me and I asked again as we pulled into the parking space outside his apartment building.

"Hey, we don't have to come back here. You can just drop me off back on The Hill. Seems like you are upset with me."

Suddenly, he turned to me and with a raised voice: "Jesus, Sophie! Don't be ridiculous. You don't have to go back to The Hill. Believe it or not, every thought or feeling I have is not about you."

Unexpectedly, as if I had a mini-faucet turned on in my eyes, I feel my tears welling up and begin streaming down my face. I was caught off guard by his reaction and his words cut deep into me.

"Oh, for Christ's sake, now you are crying?! Women are so ridiculous sometimes. Just because I said I wasn't thinking of you? Okay, fine. I was thinking of Sarah! I get to think about her sometimes, you know. Sorry, but you aren't the only one I have had feelings for. She broke my heart, Sophie, and now she is probably out with some guy about to get laid. I can feel bad about that. He's probably a guy she already cheated on me with anyway. Stupid whore."

I feel like I can't breathe and realize that as I try to find words to say something, I can't. I am holding my breath. I wait, breathe out slowly, and try to take a deep breath in. Finally I say, "I am sorry. I had no idea you felt so hurt about her. I thought you were over her. Sorry I was so selfish tonight."

Looking more sad than angry, he hugs me and whispers against my cheek. "Thank you so much. You have no idea how much it means to me that you apologized to me. Sarah never felt sorry for anything. I am over her. I love you. It's just that I still feel hurt by some of things she did to me. That's all."

Kissing my cheek, then my neck, he begins to massage my back, working his way around to my breasts. "Sophie, I need to have you right now. Let's get inside."

We quickly make our way into his apartment and even though I am still feeling light-headed from all the beer and his sudden outburst that took place in the last half hour, I oblige his advances. I let him take all my clothes off and take my hands to begin removing his as well. He carries me into his bedroom and tosses me onto the bed. Immediately and aggressively, he begins having sex with me.

"Ow!" I shout out as he pushes down on me harder and deeper. "Stop! You're hurting me." He keeps going and I push him away as hard as I can. He stops as if I have just punched him in the face. He looks puzzled.

"I'm sorry, Sophie. I didn't mean to hurt you." He rolls off of me and tears begin rolling down his face. "What the hell is wrong with me?"

I find that I can't say anything again. I am not sure if he actually wants a response or not. Not even sure he is asking a question at this point. I slowly get up and let him know I am going to take a quick shower.

"Fine," he says apathetically.

After standing under the hot stream of water for a few minutes, I begin to relax. Then the bathroom lights go out and a soft, golden glow fills the room. Ollie's father joins me in the shower. "Oh, Sophie, I am so sorry I am screwing up tonight."

"It's okay," I assure him. "I understand heartbreak, too. It can be messy and inconvenient, can't it?"

"Sure can," he says as he gives me another hug. Slowly, he begins to massage my shoulders and back with the soap and I feel myself relax even more. It feels good to be in a softer, gentler space with him again. I turn to kiss him and he abruptly stops me after my first kiss.

"No. Listen, let's just shower and turn this night around. I think sex is out for the night."

I feel a little hurt and rejected. I somberly turn and step out of the shower and onto the rug to dry off. "No problem," I say quietly.

"What's the matter now?" He asks irritably.

"Nothing. It's just been a weird night. I wasn't trying to have sex with you. I just wanted to feel close to you and thought a kiss would be okay. I was wrong."

He stares at me as if there were three heads resting on my shoulders.

"Wow! You are such a bitch! Clearly this has been a hard night for me and I have a lot on my mind. Sarah obviously, and now this about how I ruined our night, even after you apologized for being so insensitive. Guess that didn't mean anything, did it? Just because I didn't do or say what you wanted?"

As he continues to yell at me, I quickly get dressed and grab my purse. This man is crazy. Absolutely nuts. I grab the phone and call Kat to come pick me up. He takes the phone gently away from me and begins sobbing heavily as he pulls me into his arms.

"I can't do this." I push him away and walk out his door. Kat is there in ten minutes and drives me up to The

Hill. Kat, wisely, doesn't say a word. The whole time, I pray he would not come after me. There is only one main road back through town and to The Hill. There is no sign of him. Once we reach the house, I hug Kat and quietly enter the house. I tiptoe up the old stairs to my bedroom. It's 2 a.m. before I collapse, exhausted.

By 7 a.m., the phone is ringing. He was crying and apologizing for being such a jerk. I can barely understand what he is saying and agree to meet him outside in a few minutes. When he arrives, he rushes out and hugs me and begs for me to forgive him. He recognizes how wrong his behavior was and tells me over and over again that he will never do that again.

"I know I need to get some help with my anger and grief, Sophie. I thought I was more over the break-up than I was. Sarah and I were together a long time, like you and Aidan, except we had been engaged and planning our wedding when things fell apart. I am so sorry I brought you into my mess."

Looking at him so sad, so insightful, and clearly vulnerable, I hug him and assure him that I am there for him.

"Oh, my God, thank you so much for understanding, Sophie. I promise I will never call you a name again."

7 p.m.

Jori

"*I* am not sure what to say, Grandma. That is horrible that my grandfather would do that."

Saddened by what she has heard, Jori pulls Dan closer and says, "I am so glad you have never done that or would do that."

"I am too, Jori." Dan hugs her.

I don't understand a man who feels compelled to put his partner down like that even though I certainly understand feeling angry, misunderstand or hurt.

The back porch overlooking the orchard grows silent. Aidan says nothing but continues to hold my grandmother close to him. Which, of course, says what I presume is on his heart and mind, like it is with ours. It's sad to think of my grandmother being spoken to in that way. Sad that another human being would want to talk to anyone like that, especially someone he or she claims to love.

Breaking the silence, I decide to ask, "So, Grandma, you stayed with my grandfather for sixteen years? Dare I hope that means he really never did call you names again? That he did deal with his issues related to What's Her Name? Sarah?"

Seeing my grandmother look up with a pain in her eyes I have never seen on her or anyone else before, I realize I have struck a deep wound and that most likely the response I get is not what I hope for. What any of us hope.

"No, I can't say he kept his promise. I can't even say our relationship didn't get worse. Much worse. Please don't think I didn't plan or dream of leaving him many, many times. I did. And I actually ended our relationship more times than I can count. Somehow, some way, he would convince me to give him another chance, to look more deeply at how I created our situation, and how I too had issues that needed to be worked on. In a way, I had become brainwashed into thinking I deserved what he did and that I was just as bad as he was.

Sophie continues. "The few people who knew what was really going on begged me to leave him and tried to point out I was better than the abuse he inflicted on me and ultimately, Ollie as well. I agreed at times, but as Maggie Grace said once: 'You will leave him for good when you realize that you can be loved without being hurt like this. He will no longer be able to abuse you once you stop believing that you deserve it'."

"She was right. But for more reasons than I want to get into right now, I stayed. I was convinced that if I just loved him enough, became more attuned to his needs, that I could manage his mood swings, his volatility, his masterful ability to be cruel in an instant, by being better.

"My denial didn't just grow from some old wound about my father's sudden departure from my life or my break-up with Aidan or any other wound I had not deeply explored in psychotherapy. It was part of a collective denial about his behavior. I couldn't accept that anyone would do what Ollie's father was doing, so I kept trying to change myself."

Sophie sighs, then goes on with her story. "When the abusive situations began to be more frequent, I reached out to one of his close friends, Matt. I realized on some level that it was not just about me, that there had to be someone else who had experienced or saw what I was seeing. Matt assured me that Ollie's father had always had problems with anger and that indeed Sarah hadn't done him any favors in the way she had treated him.

"Matt admitted that Ollie's father had done some horrible things to Sarah, and agreed that they didn't justify what she had done to him. I even reached out to his mother once and she swiftly 'corrected' my accusatory implication that he was the source of the problem. She too, talked about the wake of devastation Sarah had left on her son and felt that he was doing what he needed to do to heal from that.

"She told me in no uncertain terms that I just needed to be more understanding and of course, look at how I contributed to his behavior. She pointed out how other women in his life had always hurt him and explained the deep wound that he carried from not having a father that knew how to show affection well.

"These interactions only solidified my denial about the impact that the abuse was having on me and drove me to work harder on being everything he had once said I was. Perfect. His soul mate. Everything he had ever wanted if only I would just...not push him to talk when he didn't want to. Not be so insecure when he talked about Sarah or wanting to do his own thing most of the time.

"After three years of trying to have a baby, we decided it was not meant to be. I mourned the idea of never being a mother, but also was relieved that I didn't have the extra responsibility. Physically, I was exhausted most of the time. I had gained about fifty pounds since we began our relationship and began to drink nightly. I didn't see it as a reaction to the abuse, but just another example of how flawed I was and how I had to try harder to be better."

"Grandma, I can't believe this. I can't believe you went through all that. Where were Auntie Maggie Grace and Great-Grandma?" Jori asks emphatically.

"Oh, they were as supportive as they could be. They couldn't make me leave or see what I wasn't ready to see. I'm sure there were times when they wanted to bang their heads in frustration, but they patiently stood by me for the first few years. I will get into that later.

"Don't forget, Jori, Kat was in my life, too. She never stopped helping me. Ever. I will be eternally grateful for that. Try to keep in mind that I was shutting down and had cut myself off from most people or things I liked because I was so tired. My life had almost entirely revolved around Ollie's father and his needs and moods. Always trying to anticipate what he might do and how to handle it. Good or bad.

"I lived for the 'honeymoon' periods. Everything would be calm and sweet and loving between us. Those were the times that came after the tension built and the blow-up occurred. Although the 'honeymoon,' of course, never lasted and the tension would begin again. In a way, trying to get back to the honeymoon was addictive. I sometimes wondered if his mother was right, that I somehow contributed to his behavior.

"One therapist told me that in abusive situations, usually the victim will unconsciously accelerate a blow-up when she senses the tension build. In this way, she feels she has some control and can prepare for when things explode. It is like a pressure gauge being released slowly to prevent a much bigger explosion."

"So you had some counseling, too?" Jori asks. "Is that how you finally stopped being with my grandfather?"

Sighing, Sophie hangs her head a little lower. "No, I wish I could say that is what did it. I had begged Ollie's father to go with me to counseling so we could work on 'our' issues. I had gotten scared after he had shoved me a couple of times and informed me that he could do much worse to me if I didn't get 'my shit together.' After punching holes in walls and breaking things around the house to further emphasize his point, I knew I needed help. Professional help.

"He went with me a few times, but after each joint session, he would get angrier. Sometimes right away or a few days would pass and he would pick a fight with me. Crazy as it might sound, I was convinced I could still make it right. That I could love him more and get us back to the place we had been when we first started dating, when the good times seemed to last longer. After a year, I realized that I was very wrong and with help from my therapist and domestic abuse advocates I began to make my safety plan.

"I started to draw and write more. I began to feel that spark ignite inside me, even if it was just a flicker. I started running again and lost about ten pounds. I didn't challenge anything Ollie's father said or did, and found ways to stay extra busy helping my mother on The Hill. At that point, I had also started to work with Maggie Grace on creating her dream of opening a bed and breakfast. One of the local farmers had decided to sell his land and the old house that stood on the property. Apparently, he had no heirs who wanted to keep the farming legacy going and he had been struggling to keep the land and farm out of financial ruin. By the time Maggie Grace was ready to put her plans to work, he was willing to sell the house, which needed a lot of work, and thirty acres of land for a steal.

"It was perfect timing for all of us. It was also about that time I found out I was pregnant with Ollie. Now more than ever, I had to find a way to make my life work. With the money I had tucked away to get my own apartment, I took Ollie's father on a weekend getaway to let him know the good news about the baby, and even purchased him a watch monogrammed with his initials. The rest I deposited in our joint checking and told him it was a gift from my mother for baby things. Fifteen hundred dollars gone. I gave my 'freedom money' away to jump-start our relationship. Flatly, I told myself that new dreams awaited.

"With the money now gone, I was almost completely dependent on him. Once again, my art work was put on the back burner. I was getting more and more depressed, but I used my mother as an excuse to stay away from Ollie's father, stating that she needed my help at the orchard. The truth was I had little to no creativity left in me. My spark went out."

Aiden reaches across to stroke Sophie's cheek, then gestures for her to go on.

"As much as I occasionally felt that creative spark flicker, it was getting harder to feel anything. I was what they refer to as 'the living dead.' I got up every day, carried out my responsibilities on The Hill. Before my pregnancy, I had drank myself to sleep every night so that the emotional pain wouldn't seep in. With the baby inside, I couldn't even turn to alcohol anymore.

"I felt desperate. So I ate. I had to have something to soothe me. Late-night treats and enormous meals temporarily soothed my spirit. I blamed the pregnancy for my rapid weight gain. I ate normally throughout the day as to not draw any suspicion from anyone and went to specialty shops sometimes twenty-five miles away to buy and store my secret food treats. I put on such a good front that I lost touch with who I was. I became the happy, expectant mother.

"Don't misunderstand me. I was happy to be having a baby and the chance to be a mother, but with it came a steep price. Now Ollie's father would have more to hold over my head. I couldn't just pack my things and go. Another little being was going to be dependent on me and legally, I couldn't take the baby and run unless it was practically a life or death situation. Even if I survived Ollie's father's wrath, he would most likely get visitation rights, regardless of how dangerous he was to my well-being.

"So denial became my alcohol, as was food. It helped that Ollie's father was brilliant at complimenting me every chance he got when others were around. Often, he was very affectionate, sweet, and gentle to me when observers were present. I loved those times and they sustained me enough to keep going. Now that I was pregnant, it couldn't just be about me anyway. More than ever, I felt I had to make the marriage work."

Aidan pulls away from Sophie and stands up slowly. "I need to take a break. I am sorry, Sophie, but it hurts so much to hear this. I can't understand why you stayed so long with someone like that, Sophie. Did I hurt you that badly?"

Aidan begins weeping. Dan and I get up to hug him as Grandma begins crying, too.

"Of course, you didn't hurt me that badly, Aidan. It was something in me that felt I deserved such punishment. Please don't think it was you and what happened between us. Aidan, you were the best person I had ever been with," Sophie assures Aiden.

In an attempt to deflect the tension and lighten the sadness in the room, Sophie adds, "You weren't perfect, Aiden, but you were the best. Just because it didn't work out between us doesn't mean that you caused me to be with someone like Ollie's father. Don't be so silly. Really."

"She's right, Aidan." Dan says. "No man should treat a woman, or anyone, like he treated Sophie. Not ever. None of us should forget that it was his choice to hurt her and continue to hurt her. Not his childhood heartaches or a line of alleged crappy women he had been with. He, like the rest of us, could have learned from our experiences and use it for doing good or bad. He chose to control, abuse, and degrade another human soul. That is his cross to bear and his alone."

Jori snuggles against Dan's broad chest, loving him so for his gentle nature and kind soul.

Wiping his tears, Aidan turns to hug Sophie. "I am so sorry to hear what he did and what happened to the woman I loved."

"Thank you, Aidan. It was a very dark time in my life and one that will always be a part of me. My experience with Ollie's father was just that. An experience. I never let it be the entire story of how I lived and who I was. It was through the pain that I began to appreciate and learn about myself after the night he almost took my life. I then decided to rewrite my story and realized once again that life is a dance. I knew I would determine what type of dance that was, but first, I had to believe I was meant to be here. I had a right to be here.

Sophie takes a deep breath. "I survived for a reason. I was *meant to dance*. I am so glad that the Sophie you fell in love with, the young girl and woman I am, can still be seen today. That is all I have ever hoped after Ollie's father left and I realized I was finally free."

Everyone sits down and without words, we know what will come next. We will learn where Ollie's father went and how Sophie found her way back again.

8 p.m.

Sophie

*J*ori and Dan, as well as Aiden, look at Sophie, awaiting
the next part of her story. Sophie squares her shoulders
and drifts off, recalling the details about the last day she
was with Ollie's father.

* * * * *

*L*ook at your left foot, big toe. What the hell kind of
divine guidance is that?! After sitting for an hour,
which is far more than I can usually spare with Ollie running
around. I am irritated. Very. Grandma had told me to get
quiet and ask for a message to be spoken to me. She said my
spirit guides were constantly trying to help me, but I kept
the noise in my head so busy with to-do lists that I never
heard their guidance.

So I thought I would try it. And of course it makes
absolutely no sense whatsoever. I call up Grandma and
demand to know what the hell *look at your left foot, big toe*
means.

"How would I know, Sophie? It's not my message and
it isn't my foot, now is it?" Grandma responds. I can almost
feel her grinning on the other end of the phone.

Even more frustrated, I hang up and stare outside as
Ollie runs around the yard, pretending he is on a pirate ship

fighting the pirates who are threatening to take his gold and food. He is so happy, thank goodness.

I seem to have protected him from knowing much about how his father treats me. From time to time, Ollie is on the receiving end of his father's impatience and even anger, but for some reason his father stops short of crossing a line with Ollie and retreats.

Of course, later, when we're alone and Ollie's in his bed, I become the proverbial punching bag and outlet for his rage. I am to blame for Ollie's unwillingness to want to spend time with him, for Ollie's wimpy tendencies and issues like his being afraid of the dark.

After ten years of Ollie being on this beautiful, green earth, there isn't much I am not to blame for when things go wrong with Ollie. At least, that is what his father tells me. To everyone else, I am a wonderful mother, loving, tough, and incredibly committed to raising a child who develops into a good person. Not famous. Not rich. Just good.

Today turned out to be like any other time when Ollie didn't do exactly what his father wanted, which was to give him a hug as soon as he got home. Ollie's father had been gone for three days on business. Even when he was home, Ollie was almost always ignored. Ollie learned early on that interrupting or challenging his father was not going to yield a positive result and so over time, Ollie learned to stay away from him (much like me) until he was summoned for one reason or another.

For tonight, I made plans for Ollie to stay at his friend's house because his father told me he would be gone until tomorrow and I wanted to spend time with Kat and Maggie Grace, to have a little "me" time. Ollie's overnight bag was already packed and so I had the unfortunate task of having to carefully find just the right words to let his father know Ollie was staying at a friend's.

I would not tell him that I had made plans, too. Perhaps if I could convince him how great it would be for the two of us to have a date night, it would minimize any sort of negative reaction he might have to Ollie not being interested in spending time with him.

I carefully approached Ollie's father as he was unpacking his travel bag, dumping his dirty clothes on the floor in a heap.

"Hey, nice to have you back. I thought you weren't coming home until tomorrow."

"Yeah, I thought so, too, but the conference got done quicker than I thought and I decided to come home and see my wife and son, but apparently he is not interested in me."

"Well, you know he is getting older and wants to spend more and more time with his friends. It is not much different for me when you're gone (*I lie*). It's just a developmental thing. Try not to take it too personally."

"Yeah, okay. Easy for you to say. You see him all the time, while I work my butt off to keep this house and everything else you both want going. Some thanks I get."

I know this is a set-up for a bigger argument, so I quickly work to redirect his disappointment about Ollie's sleepover. Ollie and I both know his mood it isn't really about us anyway. Whatever Ollie's father had hoped he would do didn't work out and we were his consolation prize.

"Listen, why don't we go to one of our favorite restaurants tonight and figure out a way we can all do something special together tomorrow? Whether he likes it or not," I say with a small laugh and a quick wink.

"Not a bad idea, surprisingly. Okay, I'll take a quick shower and you can drop that little shit off. Maybe when he realizes how much he hurt me he won't ignore me the next time I come home early just to see him."

I stand on my tiptoes to kiss him on the cheek. "Sounds like a plan."

Walking away from him, I feel sick to my stomach. He is the last person I want to be with tonight and I will warn Ollie about his father's frame of mind so we have a plan to keep things peaceful tomorrow.

Quickly, I call Maggie Grace to let her know that Ollie's father came home unexpectedly early and I am going out on a date with him. I tell her I am sorry, but will see her and Kat tomorrow. I make sure she knows that Ollie is at the Jacobson's house for the night. In fact, he will be right next to Maggie Grace's house should he not be able to reach us. I always have options for Ollie to call if he needs to reach me.

It is also part of my safety plan for everyone to know where I am and how to use the phone tree to discover if anything is amiss should I not show up where I need to be If we were fighting and I knew I needed help, I could confidently explain to him that Maggie Grace was on her way; if I didn't let her know, she might walk in on us fighting, which I knew he didn't want her to see.

Anyone, period. He liked the charade he put on. It was his way of reminding me that he could control himself if he wanted to, but didn't need to because clearly, I deserved some sort of punishment. He would decide when and how much the "disciplinary action" lasted.

By the time this night arrived, I had been with him for over fifteen years. During that time, he had choked me twice, told me that he would put me through a wall if I tried to take Ollie, and threatened to kills us because I was such an awful person. Besides, he told me, "No one will believe you, Sophie. You are depressed and drink too much. You are so stupid. You think I don't know about your self-medicating? It won't be hard to convince a family court judge that you're an alcoholic. Do you honestly think a family court judge won't give a reputable addictions counselor full custody after he/she learns what you are? You really are a piece of work."

Those words literally scared me straight. I hadn't had a drop to drink in over six years. I knew it was just a matter of time before he actually tried to kill me.

After dropping Ollie off at his friend's house and letting Maggie Grace know where I was so she could alert the others, I arrive home to find Ollie's father drinking a beer.

"You look so handsome! Let me run upstairs and change real quick so I don't look so sloppy next to you."

"Okay, Hot Stuff, hurry up. I'm starving," he calls back.

I quickly scan my closet and find a simple navy-blue dress. It is one of Ollie's father's favorites and mine, too. I grab my spaghetti-strapped heels and hurry back downstairs. I know Ollie's father doesn't like to wait. Interestingly enough, I never know how long is too long.

As soon as my foot reaches the last step, I feel a crushing pain in my left foot as Ollie's father's stomps down hard on top of it.

"What's this?!" He shoves the phone and caller ID in my face. It is too close to read.

"What do you mean?" I ask in a panicked voice, trying not to throw up from the pain in my foot. I am fairly certain he has broken it.

"This!" He screams. Then in a mocking tone, he recites the voice mail from Maggie Grace about how I had to cancel our plans to go out with Ollie's father.

In my mind, I start rapidly computing every word I said. Is there anything she might said that could have tipped him off that I didn't want to go with him? I think I erased her message. I quickly surmise that is not the case. I didn't slip up. What the hell is going on?

My voice cracks as I try to ask again what he is talking about. For some reason, I can't hide my nervousness.

"You made plans? That's what! How am I ever going to trust you if you act like someone who can't be trusted? When I am away, do you do whatever the hell you want? I thought you just sat around doing jigsaw puzzles and justifying why your sorry ass can't work just so you can stay home and care for Ollie. I guess the real deal is that you just want time to go out drinking with your sister and your dumb slut friend, Kat."

This infuriates me. Something inside of me starts to snap. With great restraint and clenched teeth, I say, "I am not in this marriage to ask your permission to spend time with my sister and my oldest friend. I haven't so much touched a drop of alcohol in years, not that I need to answer to you!" I point to the beer on the counter. "Real rich coming from an addictions counselor who drinks every night he's home with his wife and kid! IF he is even home to do that!"

He grabs my neck and pushes me forcefully onto the couch. "This is my goddam house! My goddam money and I will decide exactly how you spend it and who you spend it with!" he screams.

I run over to where he had thrown the phone, grab it up, and race toward the kitchen. I rapidly begin hitting the keys for 9-1-1. But before I can talk, he grabs my arm and drags me back to the front room. He picks up the side table and swings it around, hitting me on my side. I can't help but howl in pain and fall heavily to the floor, clutching my arm close to me.

The last thing I remember is him saying in an eerily calm voice: "You are a waste of life. An absolute fucking waste of life, Sophie." My head is numb and everything goes pitch black.

Three days later, I wake up in a hospital room with my mother, Maggie Grace, Kat, and Ollie around me.

They tell me Ollie's father had taken the side table and slammed it down on my head as I stumbled to get back up and run. The blow knocked me unconscious, but somehow I was aware enough to hold up the arm he hadn't hurt, which fortunately reduced the impact. I ended up having a small hairline fracture and swelling in my brain. Because of the car accident I had years ago, my brain was traumatized more than had it been if it was my first injury.

The doctors told my family I was lucky to be alive. Either injury could have killed me. And my left foot and left big toe were broken.

I guess my spirit guides were actually trying to tell me something. Fortunately, the foot and toe would heal, as would my head injury. I would walk away with some discomfort in my foot and have some memory issues only. I was one of the lucky ones, they said.

That night, Ollie's father took off when he saw me on the floor, motionless. He was presumed dead when his car was found in the Greenhill River, even though his body was never recovered. The police investigators closed the case and labeled it an accidental drowning. Ollie received his father's Social Security benefits and the trust that had been in his father's name from Ollie's great-grandparents. It was the best thing his father ever gave him. An opportunity to attend college for free.

Sadly, Ollie didn't miss his father any more than he would have had the man been alive. He has always mourned the father he never would have. One who showed love and affection without conditions. No longer having to be afraid of him actually helped him permanently move on from grieving a father he had always wished for.

As I worked on my own recovery—physically, psychologically and emotionally—I read through the journals I had kept over the years. Initially, I was drawn to the ones I had written when I was with Ollie's father. Part of my healing was to dispel the lies Ollie's father tried to make me believe.

From the information I gathered from my actual journals, he called me names 786 times (I counted), shoved me three times—one of the times, I hit my head against a bookshelf, which made me dizzy—choked me twice, humiliated me in public more times than I care to admit, often shouting and reprimanding me for some imagined transgression, told me to get the fuck out of his life 27 times, threw his wedding ring across the room more than a dozen times, threatened that he could kill me three times if he wanted, threatened to cause me severe bodily harm five times, and threatened to kill himself at least four times because I was so crazy it was the only way to get away from me.

I had even written about a time when he actually admitted he had been far worse to Sarah. That I should be lucky I got him when I did, because she had been with him when he was much angrier. At least he hadn't cheated on me like he had when he was with her.

These scenes were only what I had written. Others that replayed in my head were often too painful to even write down.

Six months after Ollie's father was presumed dead, I never looked at another journal in which I had written about him. I had had enough pain and didn't want to keep reliving it.

With Maggie Grace's and my mother's help, I slowly began to live again. That was one of the greatest gifts of all. You see, MG and my mother had grown so frustrated with me because I wouldn't leave him. So they distanced themselves and as Ollie's father's abuse continued, he actually began recruiting them as his allies. He had them convinced enough that I was not so perfect and wonderful and that although he had crossed a line or two with me, they didn't really know just how angry I could get. Just how afraid he had become of me. I don't think they ever believed him fully, but it was enough to question me and keep the distance between us.

It broke my heart.

I later learned in my counseling that it is common for abusive men to alienate their partners by playing victim to her friends and family. Often they use a weak moment against them, when after days and hours of being demeaned, sworn at, called names and threatened, that the woman breaks and either becomes enraged or withdraws and becomes hysterical. Really, the hysteria is a panic attack of sorts, a break in one's psyche between what is real and not real.

That is the moment an abused woman realizes she is completely consumed by fear. Living in terror of never knowing when he might be nice or lash out. Her friends, her family, and his family become allies, and she is even more isolated from any support.

The more depressed I became, the more I self-medicated, cried endlessly for hours about how badly I felt about him, the more fuel I gave him to solidify his victim story to others.

It was a game he won over and over again, with my deepening isolation, fear, and whittling down any self-esteem I had or tried to have. He treated my degradation like a personal achievement.

The "gas lighting," manipulation, and attempts to make me think *I* was the crazy one, were the hardest parts of being with Ollie's father. He was so good at it that I even got caught up in his sophisticated mind games. How could I expect anyone else to see it if I couldn't?

I lived with him daily. Who would believe me after I became his number-one cheerleader regarding how poorly Sarah treated him, how he had endured so much in life, and how hard he worked to be the professional that he was.

Who would believe me after I shouted at him that he was the worst person I had ever been with, that he was a psycho asshole, and that I hated him. Somehow, those infrequent psychic breaks were labeled "abusive" and I was no different than he was. It didn't matter that such behavior was a regular pattern for him, but not for me. It didn't matter that I never threatened or actually hurt him like he had me.

One night, out of desperation, I called her—Sarah. I had tracked her phone number down years before, but never had the courage to actually reach out to her. When we finally spoke, she said, "I have been waiting for your call." I was stunned.

I began sobbing uncontrollably sobbing. She waited patiently and through her own tears, she said, "I'm so sorry you know this pain, too."

We talked about how Ollie's father used our weakest moments to justify his behaviors. His compliments to others about us at times were our cue to smile and appreciate what he was doing for us.

Sarah revealed his repeated inquiry. "How abusive could I be?" he would ask. "Everyone knows how much I love you. Do you think anyone would believe your exaggerated ideas of who I am to you? I am not some monster."

After I physically recovered from that night, I had a very long journey recovering from within. The hardest part became loving and accepting myself as a person who had the right to be here. No names he called me were as damaging as the way he treated me, as if I didn't have a right to be who I was. To live creatively, passionately, stumbling through life, flawed. I tried to be the best person I could be. He solidified this wound the night he told me I was "a waste of life."

I had been living a very dangerous game of cat and mouse. One I almost didn't survive.

8 p.m.

Aidan

I admit I was not prepared to hear Sophie share her journey through the years we weren't together. I never imagined her life would have gone the way that it did. Of course, she didn't either. I don't know how to comfort her. It doesn't feel like enough. I know she would say that wasn't true, but I can't help but feel that way.

Why hadn't I reached out to her? Why did it take all this time for me to muster the courage to see her? I don't know if I will ever have the answer. I don't even know if it matters as much as what I hope that Sophie and I can do together now.

"Sophie, I can't help but ask why you stayed with that man so long. How did you keep going?" I ask.

Sighing with a deep, mournful look, Sophie begins to explain to me that the "why's" were endless.

"It was hard to give up on him. On what I had dreamed I would have with him. Believe it or not, I really loved him. I kept telling myself that he wasn't always abusive. There were some really great moments and some sweet memories I was able to access from time to time in my mind. Those got me through the tougher moments, but it also kept me stuck in the abusive pattern with him.

"Getting back to those 'good times' was addictive for me. I knew his cycle and sometimes couldn't wait for the explosion as the tension heightened, because inevitably the good moments would come rushing back. Sometimes the honeymoon period lasted weeks.

Quietly, I say, "Sophie, you don't need to go on if it's too hard."

She makes a dismissive motion with her hand and continues. "As much as he did to me, I added to the pain by giving up on myself. Relinquishing my voice, my own personal truths, intensified my pain and depression. Once I became a participant in his abuse toward me, I lost valuing myself and ultimately my willingness to live.

"I believe that night occurred because I had given up. Thanks to whatever divine source, I lived and was given another chance to rewrite my story. Fortunately, mine was not a physical death, but rather a spiritual one. The Sophie I had become or believed I had become by staying with him, died that night. The woman who awakened in that hospital room three days later was the Sophie you always knew and sits with all of you today."

I reach across to gently caress the only woman I have ever truly loved.

"Hearing myself say that almost makes it seem like it was a quick process or even an easy journey. Although I had more awareness, it wasn't either of those, of course. It took many months and a few years of small steps to help me get to a better place.

"By the time Ollie was in high school, I was just getting to a place where I no longer startled awake every hour or two, convinced I could hear Ollie's father walking on the maple hardwood floors downstairs. It didn't matter that I no longer lived in the house we once shared. I had brought my wounds, fears, shame, and anxiety with me to The Hill.

Isolation, when you are working on these kinds of issues, is the enemy. I survived with a lot of help.

"It was the hardest inside job I ever had to do, but I managed. Each breath I took was a reminder that I could make it. I was breathing for a reason and at the end of each day, that is all that mattered.

As Maggie Grace and my mother helped me along, I learned that they had discovered things within themselves that were healing as well. For Maggie Grace, it was her drinking and for my mother, the letting go of her heartbreak of my father leaving to have a different life. I realized then, that even in my darkest, most painful moments, I could still inspire someone to keep going. Until then, I never felt I was worth enough to inspire anyone.

"I found my way back to my art, my dreams. Eventually, I was able to open my own art studio. All my dreams were coming true. I was back and whole.

"Aiden, I can't say my years with Ollie's father were wasted time. Each year he was gone, I felt more alive. I realized from that experience that I didn't have to be the perfect person, mother, sister, or daughter. I just had to be me."

I say in a calm, soft voice, "Thank you, Sophie, for sharing all of this. I don't know if I had a right to ask, but I am glad I did. I never thought I would learn as much I have as an old man. You are truly the most beautiful person I have ever known."

Hugging one another and settling into an embrace that is comfortable on the sofa, Sophie and I begin preparing ourselves for the next step in our journey.

Sophie

"Jori, follow your heart no matter what. It is the only way back to love. Take your time, but not too long. Let Aidan and me be a reminder to not waste time with your pride and forgetting the one thing we could count on most—love. Love for ourselves and for what we shared together. For too long, I lived my life always hoping that someone or something would give me the answers on how to live. Only I could do that for myself.

"Dear girl, if I have any regrets, it would be losing sight of valuing myself and thinking I didn't have the answers from within. Without love for yourself, you have nothing. No one can give you what you don't have within your own deepest parts of your spirit.

"Thank you so much for sharing your story, Grandma."

She hugs me and I watch tearful, sweet Jori waddling to the kitchen to get Dan.

Aidan and I turn to one another, knowing it is time for us to leave.

"Let's get going, Sophie," Aidan says quietly.

Breathing in the late summer's evening air, Aidan helps me to my feet.

"Please wait here for a second, so I can tell Jori we are heading out to the orchard."

Walking through the kitchen, Sophie leans into the entryway of her library to tell Jori, "I think Aidan has something he wants to show me before the rain comes."

"What rain?" Jori says, peering through the window. "The sky is clear and in fact, it's the perfect kind of evening to walk under the stars without having to worry about getting wet."

"Well, then, I guess we won't get wet then."

"Okay, Grandma, but make sure you two come back soon. I want us to have some tea before we go to bed. This has been such a long, great day for me and Dan.

* * * * *

*H*olding one another's hands, Sophie and Aidan step out into the evening. The air smells of apples, pine and maple leaves that are preparing to turn orange, yellow, and red in the coming weeks.

"Why do I feel you might be up to something, Aidan?" Sophie says, smiling.

"Perhaps it is because I have been thinking about a day like this one ever since I saw you at Willow Lake all those years ago."

"What is it?" Sophie asks excitedly and a bit impatient.

"Well, I can't wait either, Sophie. It has definitely been a long time to wait for one of the best days of your life, hasn't it?"

"Has it really been that long?" Sophie asks with a wink. Kissing her gently on the lips, Aiden leads Sophie to the path she has walked so many times before.

* * * * *

I feel like a young girl again, about to go on an adventure. Walking barefoot on the softened grass I can smell the wonderful aroma of the earth filling my lungs. There are just enough openings in the canopy of trees to see the stars dotting the sky like a thousand sparkles. The moon is full and bright, providing us just enough light to walk. Holding Aidan's hand as he leads me toward our tree, I look ahead and see something sparkling down the path, but I can't tell what it is quite yet.

* * * * *

"*A*idan?" Sophie says softly.

Gently rubbing Sophie's arm to reassure her that everything is just fine, Aidan says, "Shhh, Sophie we are almost there." Taking a few more steps and flashing to the night in the snowy trees so many years ago, Sophie's eyes begin to water, pools of tears bringing brief sweet memories.

"Okay, close your eyes, Sophie, ole girl, and I will take you the rest of the way."

"All right, Aidan, but you'd better not let me trip! I am an old woman now, remember? I must really trust you," Sophie says with a smile.

"I hope so, Sophie, after all this time. And by the way, when did you get old?"

Walking for what feels like hours, Sophie senses the air change around her body. It is suddenly warmer, as if the sun has come back out. Goose bumps of anticipation rise on her arms. What does Aidan have waiting for her?

"Okay, Sophie, we are here."

* * * * *

Turning me gently toward him and holding me close enough for me to feel his breath warmly pass over my cheek, he says, "Okay, you can open your eyes now."

Slowly raising my lids, I find myself encircled in every direction by beautiful sparkling silver and golden lights. I am overwhelmed by the sight. The silent tears that had started earlier now flow down my face in a steady, slow stream.

Placing my hand on my heart, I sob. Sob for all the times I missed Aidan and couldn't hold him. For all the times I struggled to find my way back to the person I was when I wasn't able to be with him. For so long, I prayed that I would feel love again. It took longer than I expected, but standing under these lights and our tree, I realize that great love always finds you again.

Gently kissing away my tears, Aidan envelops me with a hug and we begin to dance.

Jori

"This has been an incredible day, don't you think, Dan?"

"Absolutely. I never expected it to turn out this way. I never imagined hearing their story would make me look so deeply into mine. Into ours."

"I know what you mean, Dan. I guess I always thought if something was meant to be, it would somehow be easy and the pieces would just all fall into place. I guess that is what happens when you don't listen to that inner voice and you get caught up in ego."

Hugging Jori, Dan asks, "Where are those two, anyway?"

"Great question," Jori says, slight concern flashing in her eyes. "They said they were going out for a walk before the rain came. Of course, when I pointed out to Sophie that no rain was indicated, her eyes told me, 'Just wait, Jori.' "

Peering out the window and then deciding to step out onto the porch to see if Sophie and Aidan were heading back toward the house, we don't see anything at first. The sky is turning a deep cobalt blue as the stars illuminate the canopy over our orchard.

Grandma knew Aiden would return to her when they were both ready. I was so thrilled to meet him today and hear their stories. Some I had heard and others of course, I had not.

I am the only Apple Tree Warrior left now, until of course, our baby arrives in a few weeks. Knowing this, I appreciate what Grandma Sophie gave me today, what she has always given me—the opportunity to look within for my answers and the strength to follow through when guided to take action, even if things don't always make sense.

I am saddened that Sophie is leaving me. I knew she would. She had been waiting for Aidan for so long, but I still feel unready for her departure. I suppose the only reason she had held on for even this long is so she could have this moment to be with him again. Seeing them go into the orchard to find their tree, I knew deep down she wouldn't be returning.

"There they are, Dan!" I say, pointing.

Watching them walk slowly hand in hand out past the garden, through the apple trees planted by the women of our family, to a path they walked so many times before. Back to the apple tree where they spent so much time when they were just two kids.

Dan and I notice their silhouettes in the moonlight, as if we were watching a picture slowly coming into focus. Aidan lit up "their" tree, as Sophie had done each year. Now I understand how deeply Sophie treasured that tradition and why she wasn't willing to let it go.

I always thought it was a little strange and unique that she did this, but I am not as sentimental as Grandma. Knowing more about their story, I have a different appreciation for this treasured tradition and the process she had leading up to the midnight lighting of their tree each year.

She always spent the whole day by that tree writing and sometimes drawing. For Sophie, it was a way to honor her story—their story—and what she still held so dear in her heart.

Barely breathing, Dan and I watch the two friends and lovers embrace and move into their dance. It was a moment Aiden and Sophie had been waiting for most of their lives.

* * * * *

*A*idan had taken his last earthly breath over a year ago and Sophie four years prior. Aiden had returned to Greenhill as we had planned. But he did so in spirit.

Taking in this thought, in the quickest of blinks, Dan and I can no longer identify their shapes among the millions of silver-white lights that trail golden ribbons as they gently glide upward from the orchard, over the great apple trees, and float toward the constellations above.

Crying and trembling, I rush as quickly as my swollen body will allow toward their tree.

She's gone. Really gone.

Trying to catch my breath and make sense of what Dan and I had just witnessed, I feel the first cool drop of rain on my face. I hold out my hand to catch the first sprinkles.

Louder and louder, the rain begins pounding the soft earth and blades of grass. The air smells like warm dirt and apples. Breathing in deeply, I look up toward the star-sprinkled sky.

Then I hold my arms up, palms ready to capture the rain, a lover's rain.

So who are the Apple Tree Warriors?

Since its earliest days, apple trees always sustained the O'Neill family. These noble trees have been part of their heritage for centuries. It was the matriarch Gratia's planting of the original Irish apple seeds in New England that established The Hill and the orchard. Despite tough and challenging times, apples always got the O'Neill women through.

Meant to Dance is Book 1 in the Apple Tree Warrior saga. Forthcoming books include *Maggie Grace* (Book 2) and *Gratia, The First Apple Tree Warrior* (Book 3).

Discussion Points

- What thoughts come to mind when you think about Sophie and Aidan and their story?

- Do you think Sophie was wrong to feel betrayed by Aidan?

- How much of a role do you think Sophie's father's departure had on her being with Ollie's father?

- As you read about the abuse that developed between Sophie and Ollie's father did you find yourself judging her for staying? What did you feel about Ollie's father?

- What do you think you might have done if you were Sophie?

- Did the ending surprise you? Were you expecting something different?

Some Facts about Domestic Violence

Source: www.safehorizon.org

What is Domestic Violence?
Domestic Violence is a pattern of behavior used to establish power and control over another person through fear and intimidation, often including the threat or use of violence. Other terms for domestic violence include intimate partner violence, battering, relationship abuse, spousal abuse, or family violence.

Who is Most Likely to Suffer from Domestic Abuse or Become a Victim of Domestic Violence?
Domestic violence and abuse can happen to anyone, regardless of gender, race, ethnicity, sexual orientation, income, or other factors. Women and men can be victims of domestic violence.

How Often Does Domestic Violence Occur?
1 in 4 women will experience domestic violence during her lifetime.

hy and When Does Domestic Abuse Happen?
No victim is to blame for any occurrence of domestic abuse or violence. While there is no direct cause or explanation why domestic violence happens, it is caused by the abuser or perpetrator. Domestic violence is most likely to take place between 6 pm and 6 am. More than 60% of domestic violence incidents happen at home.

Domestic Violence in America: General Statistics and Facts

- Women ages 18 to 34 are at greatest risk of becoming victims of domestic violence.

- More than 4 million women experience physical assault and rape by their partners.

- In 2 out of 3 female homicide cases, females are killed by a family member or intimate partner.

- Without help, girls who witness domestic violence are more vulnerable to abuse as teens and adults.

- Without help, boys who witness domestic violence are far more likely to become abusers of their partners and/or children as adults, thus continuing the cycle of violence in the next generation.

- #1 FACT: Most domestic violence incidents are never reported. Help change the facts. Speak up, speak out, and make a difference for victims of domestic violence.

Resources

If you or someone you know is involved in a domestic abuse situation, here are some resources for you to consider using:

National Domestic Violence Hotline:
800-799-SAFE (7233)

Crime Victims Hotline:
866-689-HELP (4357)

Rape, Abuse and Incest National Network Hotline (RAIN):
1-800-656-4673

Book Resources:
Should I Stay or Should I Go? by Lundy Bancroft and Jac Patrissi (Berkley Books, New York)

When Love Goes Wrong: by Ann Jones and Susan Schechter (Harper Perrenial)

Why Does He DO That? Inside the Minds of Angry and Controlling Men: by Lundy Bancroft (Berkley Books, New York)

It's My Life Now: by Meg Kennedy Dugan and Roger R. Hock (Routledge, Taylor & Francis Group)

There are many resources out there and I was happy to learn that I could have filled pages and pages of them for you. I chose the primary resources to help get you started. Don't wait. Talk to someone you trust. If you feel like you don't have anyone call your local police for help or call the numbers I listed above.

Acknowledgments

I am a blessed woman. There have been many people along this journey with me. Each person who has come into my life has been for a reason and although not all remain by my side today, I am grateful for having had the chance to be a part of one another's lives.

There are some people I would like to mention specifically right now for a variety of reasons. They are acknowledged by the unique ways in which I felt that they supported me as I began to rewrite my personal story.

To the families who helped me become the woman I am today: Adam and Debbie Wetzel and Nancy and Victor Olson. Inviting me to experience family without pain was one of the greatest gifts I have ever received. It directly impacted the type of person and parent I strive to be every day.

I would like to acknowledge my family of origin. Without their stories of triumph and personal struggles, I would be missing a piece of who I am and how that helps me navigate where I want to be.

To my childhood friends who did not judge the scared and often struggling young girl I was: Amy Wetzel, Jenny Olson, Rachel Ehrenberg and Catha Vesper. You were my rocks.

To my first counselor, Carol Baker, who let me pay her five dollars a week for almost two years so that I could begin healing. I am forever grateful you believed I was worth working with and for planting the seed that eventually grew into a social work career for me that has spanned the past twenty or more years.

Joanna Greenwood and Missylyn Keene, thank you for holding the space I needed to share my secrets in.

For Tammy, who listened for the many hours, often late at night, as I struggled to find my voice and self-worth again. Thank you for sharing your wisdom and your story. You inspire me to never give up, regardless of how tough it feels. You are a true friend in every way imaginable. I love you with all my heart.

Additional gratitude goes to my publisher Kira Henschel for encouraging, editing, and making this dream come true for me. She knew I had a story somewhere to tell and believed that I could tell it.

About the Author

Sonya Behan grew up in a small New England town and in a family where domestic violence was present. As she worked through her childhood trauma of not only being a witness to violence, but becoming a survivor of it as an adult, she realized she was not alone. Through professional and personal support, she was able to overcome the often debilitating effects of domestic abuse.

For more than two decades, Sonya has dedicated herself to helping others. She earned a Master's degree in Social Work and has used her art and training in Energy Healing to pay it forward to those who are experiencing abuse. She often helps others re-write their stories and reclaim the lives they always wanted.

All fictional work is autobiographical to some degree. Sonya used her personal and professional experiences to create fictional characters she believes could reach anyone who may be facing domestic abuse or knows of someone who is dealing with it.

Sonya currently resides in the Midwest with her two sons.

If you would like Sonya to visit your group, book club, or organization to talk about the ways you can help yourself or someone you know overcome domestic abuse and reclaim their lives, please contact her at :

Email: sonyabehan@gmail.com
www.sonyabehan.com (website and blog)

CPSIA information can be obtained at www.ICGtesting.com
Printed in the USA
BVOW08s1245200316

440670BV00004B/2/P